FOUR STEPBROTHERS FOR CHRISTMAS

A CONTEMPORARY REVERSE HAREM ROMANCE

K.C. CROWNE

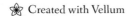

"What's the surprise, Mom?" I ask, tingling with curiosity.
"Your future step-brothers are here!"
As the door swings open, my heart lurches to a halt.
I know these men. Intimately.

Imagine a snowy holiday retreat with four captivating, successful men.
AKA the stars of your wildest fantasies.

The catch? They're your bosses.
But their eyes linger on you like you're the last of Santa's cookies.
So for seven unforgettable days you relish in all their attention and hunger.

You say your goodbyes and thank Santa for making your wildest wish come true.
But when you arrive home for Christmas you receive the most shocking news!

The men of your dreams are destined to become your future step brothers!
Now what?!?

CHAPTER 1

BECCA

"Chef Becca, would you please join us in the office?"

A deep, masculine voice that couldn't possibly belong to anyone but Isaac Tyson sounded through the kitchen intercom, adding an unplanned twist to my otherwise predictable Tuesday afternoon.

I wiped my hands on my apron, shooting a glance at the clock—3:47 PM. An odd time for a meeting, considering I'd normally be knee-deep in food prep for tomorrow. Curiosity piqued, I untied the apron and hung it on its hook before exiting the kitchen.

As I walked down the hallway, my athletic shoes silent on the marble floor. The offices of FourSight Marketing were bustling as ever, men and women in sharp, professional garb zipping around purposefully. I stuck out a like a sore thumb in my kitchen clothes, but that was more than fine with me.

I reached the door to Mr. Tyson's office quickly. I took a deep breath, put on my best professional face, and pushed it open.

All four of my bosses were there—Isaac, Vinnie, Archer,

and Luke – the heads of FourSight Marketing, a play on their joint, four-way ownership.

Each man could be a model for a different kind of cologne ad—Isaac for the sophisticated, Vinnie for the charming, Archer for the edgy, and Luke for the quietly intense. But I'd been here long enough to keep my wits about me, even in a room that could double as a GQ photo shoot.

All were impossibly sexy, tall and handsome and seemingly built in just the perfect way to drive me wild. Walking in and having four sets of eyes on me was enough to make my breath hitch, to make my pussy clench. I'd grown accustomed to the appeal of the four men since beginning my employment at FourSight, but there's only so much handsome in one room a woman can take.

Isaac sat behind his desk, leaning back in his chair. He looked like a buff version of Brad Pitt, with piercing green eyes framed by wire-rimmed glasses and short, military-style blonde hair. He was a man of few words, with an air of leadership that felt both welcoming and intimidating at once.

"Chef," Isaac began, his voice snapping me out of my thoughts. "Please, have a seat."

I took the offered chair, interested in this unexpected meeting. There was an unspoken formality in the room that seemed almost like a prelude, and I found myself both intrigued and slightly apprehensive about what would come next.

I crossed my legs and straightened my spine. "Is everything alright with the menu?"

Isaac chuckled, a sound as smooth as aged scotch. "The menu is excellent as always. We actually wanted to talk to you about something else."

Vincent, or Vinnie as he preferred, was standing next to him. He was a couple of inches taller than Isaac, with dark brown hair kept short but stylish. Of Italian descent, his features were defined yet soft, charming and approachable. He was the company's people person, always quick with a smile or a witty comment. He leaned forward in his chair, flashing his easygoing smile. "Yeah, don't worry, this isn't a critique session for your culinary skills."

In another corner of the room was Archer Gallo, silent and brooding as always, gave a nod of agreement. One of Vinnie's younger brothers, he was more rugged and beefy, with a shaved head, full-sleeve tattoos, and a well-groomed beard framing his brooding expression. Despite his tough exterior, something about his presence hinted at a highly focused, perhaps even slightly obsessive personality.

Luke, Archer's twin and ever the observer, simply met my eyes, reassuring me without words.

Isaac leaned back in his chair, interlocking his fingers as if he were carefully choosing his next words. "We'd like to extend an invitation to you to accompany us to our mountain cabin for a short retreat—five days. We want to take some time to brainstorm and strategize away from the daily distractions of the office."

I blinked, processing what he'd just said. A mountain cabin? Five days? My mind spun with questions I dared not ask out loud. Like, why couldn't these incredibly capable men cook for themselves?

"I'm assuming I'll be responsible for all the meals?" I ventured, asking for clarity.

"Exactly," Isaac nodded. "We'll cover the costs for your transportation, and in addition to your regular salary, we're offering a generous bonus for your time." He wrote something down on a piece of paper and handed it to me.

The numbers Isaac offered were, indeed, generous. Tempting. I felt a magnetic pull toward the offer, but something compelled me to establish boundaries first.

"Would I also be expected to function as a maid?" I asked, straightforward as always. "Because if so, I need to clarify that my responsibilities will begin and end in the kitchen."

Vinnie laughed softly, his eyes twinkling with amusement. "No, Chef, you won't be required to moonlight as a housekeeper. We have a cleaning crew that takes care of the place. Your domain would solely be the kitchen."

Archer shrugged when I looked at him, as if the matter were already settled in his mind. Luke nodded in agreement, his eyes meeting mine. The quiet understanding in his gaze somehow reassured me more than any words could. He was cleaner-cut than his twin, no beard, and only one visible tattoo—a tribute to their late mother, if I recalled correctly. He exuded a quieter intensity than his brothers, a subtle undercurrent of depth and perceptiveness. He always seemed to be watching, listening, as though he were perpetually gathering information and assessing situations.

I leaned back, processing. A part of me wondered what the dynamics would be like. I was used to interacting with them in professional settings, bound by the structured environment of the workplace. What would it be like in a casual, more personal setting? The thought was both intimidating and exhilarating.

As if sensing my hesitation, Isaac spoke again. "We'd completely understand if you're not comfortable with the idea, Becca. But we trust you, and honestly, we couldn't think of anyone better suited for this."

"There's more," Vinnie added.

"More?" I asked, curious.

Isaac cleared his throat. "We've been considering some company changes—expansions, actually. But for that to happen, there are certain opportunities we'll need to explore. Some of these discussions will require discretion on everyone's part, including yours."

I arched an eyebrow, intrigued but slightly bewildered. "Discretion? I'm not in the habit of sharing company secrets, if that's what you mean."

Vinnie laughed. "It's not about that. It's a bit more complicated. And it's something we hope you'd be comfortable with, but we'll need your full consent."

My heart rate picked up a notch. "I'm all ears."

Each man exchanged a look, as if passing an unspoken agreement between them. Finally, Isaac spoke.

"How would you feel about extending your current responsibilities?"

"As in, being our personal chef," Archer said, making the proposal clear. "Not only for the executive floor. You'd cook for us, travel with us, create meal plans for us – the works."

"But this would put you closer to us," Vinnie added. "And that's where the discretion comes in."

My eyes darted from one face to another. They were serious. And suddenly, the room felt a few degrees warmer.

"We would, of course, discuss the terms in detail," Isaac added. "Only if you're interested."

Interested? I was puzzled and maybe a dash flattered. But most of all, I felt the unmistakable rush of a new challenge. And for the first time in months, I felt genuinely excited about what lay ahead.

"Oh, I'm interested," I said without hesitation, locking eyes with each of them in turn. "Let's hear the details."

Truth be told, the idea of spending five days in a moun-

6 | K.C. CROWNE

tain cabin, immersed in my culinary element, was too alluring to resist. And if this was a possible way to assure my future -and career- even better.

Isaac gave a brief explanation of what was expected over the five days. I met Isaac's gaze, then Vinnie's, Archer's, and finally, Luke's. I saw varying degrees of hope and expectation in their eyes, and for some inexplicable reason, that sealed the deal.

"I accept," I announced, feeling a newfound excitement course through me.

"Excellent," Isaac said, his lips curling into a satisfied smile as the others visibly relaxed.

Luke seemed to sense my lingering questions, because as everyone began to disperse, he caught my eye and added, "You should know, Becca, when you're not actively cooking, your time is entirely your own. We want you to enjoy the place as much as we do."

Archer added, "The cabin's in a beautiful location. You could go hiking—though it might be a bit chilly this time of year. There's a hot tub, the deck has a truly amazing view you won't want to miss. Or if you'd prefer to relax indoors, your room will have all the amenities."

The way he described it made it sound like I was getting an all-expenses-paid vacation rather than a job assignment. Cooking, to me, wasn't work; it was passion, it was art. The idea that I could spend my off hours soaking in a hot tub or hiking through gorgeous scenery felt almost too good to be true.

I looked at Luke, his eyes holding that same quiet sincerity I'd come to appreciate. I realized then just how much I'd unconsciously been seeking his assurance, and how much it meant now that I had it.

"That sounds wonderful," I admitted, the last of my reservations dissipating like morning fog under the sun.

He smiled, clearly pleased. "We're glad you've agreed."

As I left the office and made my way back to the kitchen, I felt a bubbling sense of excitement, an effervescence of anticipation. The cabin trip wasn't just a business proposition; it was shaping up to be a unique sort of adventure, an opportunity to break away from the routine, to be inspired and perhaps even *to* inspire.

Maybe the mountain air and the stunning vistas would spark some culinary creativity, leading me to perfect a recipe or invent a new dish entirely. Plus, cooking for Isaac, Vinnie, Archer, and Luke—a discerning but appreciative audience—would undoubtedly be a pleasure, not a chore.

As I began to pre-plan the menus in my head, envisioning the ingredients I'd need, the flavors I could combine, and the plating aesthetics, it became increasingly clear: this trip was an incredible gift, a serendipitous alignment of work and play, of duty and desire. And I couldn't wait to see how it would unfold.

I guided my car up the narrow, serpentine road, every twist and turn demanding my full attention. The vehicle was weighed down by an impressive haul of groceries—enough to feed four large men and myself for five days, three meals a day, plus snacks. I glanced in the rearview mirror, catching a glimpse of the packed bags in the back seat, and the tension in my shoulders eased just a little.

My focus had to be on the road, especially with how steep and unpredictable the incline was, but my mind was far away, grappling with the things money could and couldn't fix. Half of the bonus had already been mentally allocated to cover my brother's next stint in rehab. This would be his third time. The other two times had torn through my savings, had borrowed hope from my already dwindling supply, yet he'd slipped back each time. Hopefully, this time would be different. Hopefully, this time he would emerge free from the demons that haunted him.

"If you can't get clean this time, Mikey, I can't keep doing this," I had told him before leaving, my voice tinged with a mixture of exasperation and sorrow. "And you won't be staying with me either. You'll have to go to Mom." The words had hurt to say, adding an emotional weight to the already heavy reality. Our mother, still blissfully ignorant of the depths of Mikey's addiction, would be a last resort. But it was a boundary I was forced to draw for my own well-being.

Shaking the melancholic thoughts from my head, I tried to focus on the road again, and just in time. Two deer bounded across the asphalt some fifty yards ahead, their forms elegant and graceful. The sight brought an involuntary smile to my face.

Finally, I saw it—the wooden sign marking the entrance to the Gallo-Tyson cabin, hidden away like some guarded secret. I exhaled, not realizing I had been holding my breath, and made the final turn into the long driveway.

As my car ascended higher, I was caught off guard by a sudden overlook. The sprawling view was just a preview of what awaited me at the cabin. My fingers itched for my camera, and I mentally catalogued the spot for a future photo session. This trip was shaping up to be a perfect blend of work and pleasure.

Finally, the road leveled off, and I pulled into the cabin's driveway. My eyes took in the architecture, the way the structure blended so seamlessly with its natural surround-ings—earthy tones, large windows, a deck that promised an undisturbed view of the world below. This would be my sanctuary for the next five days, an escape from the financial worries, the emotional fatigue, and the relentless grind of city life.

I parked and took a moment to collect myself, preparing to switch from solitary traveler to professional chef. As I looked at the cabin, a sense of calm washed over me. Here, I could indulge in what I loved most—cooking, nature, photography—without the looming shadows of my life's complexities.

The building was more like a luxurious mountain lodge than a cabin, large and inviting with huge windows that undoubtedly offered incredible views. I could already smell the pine in the air, the untouched crispness city life couldn't offer. For a moment, I just sat there, appreciating the beauty and the promise of temporary escape.

Grabbing my purse and the first load of groceries, I climbed out of the car. The cool mountain air greeted me, a stark contrast to the heated interior of the vehicle. I looked around, inhaling deeply. It was quiet—peaceful in a way only the mountains can offer.

The crisp mountain air instilled in me a surge of opti-mism. Maybe I would come back from these five days with more than a generous paycheck. Maybe I'd come back rein-vigorated, a little stronger, and a little more hopeful that things could get better, both for me and for Mikey.

CHAPTER 2

ISAAC

I stood on the front porch of our mountain cabin, coffee mug in hand, savoring the crisp morning air. The city life felt worlds away here in the Adirondacks. Before me, snow-covered mountains stretched out, their peaks bathed in a dazzling layer of fresh powder that glowed in the morning light. Towering pines dusted in snow stood sentinel, their branches heavy and still. This was peace, a kind you can't find in the boardrooms and skyscrapers, a sanctuary for both body and thought.

My eyes scanned the winding driveway. We hadn't heard from Becca since she'd headed out from the city. Her plan was to make the drive, then pick up groceries – nothing crazy, but a slight concern on these tricky mountain roads, even with the Land Rover we'd rented for her. She had our numbers, she had my credit card, and we told her dinner by evening was all that was required today.

"Still waiting for our chef?" Vinnie's voice broke through my thoughts.

I shrugged, still watching the horizon. "She should be here soon. Roads can be tricky this time of year."

Vinnie chuckled. "Ah, she'll be fine. She's not the kind of woman to be dissuaded by a little mountain drive."

True, Becca didn't strike me as the type to get side-tracked or rattled easily. I thought back to our meeting, when she'd pressed us about whether she'd be expected to clean on top of cooking and made it clear she would do no such thing. I respected that kind of no-nonsense attitude.

Yet, as much as this trip was about getting away, I couldn't entirely escape work. The next big client, the next big leap for the firm—those thoughts are never too far away. We were at a stage where the next level of success was almost within our grasp. But at what cost?

I turned up the temp on the outdoor heater, letting the warmth seep into the air. The frigid mountain air didn't bother me, but the guys would appreciate the heat when they joined me.

One by one, they emerged onto the heated porch. Archer came out first, a glass of his usual ruby red wine in hand. I couldn't help but chuckle. For a guy who looked like he could be the leader of a biker gang, Archer was an insufferable wine snob.

"What're you doing out here?" he asked, taking a sip of his Cabernet.

"Waiting on Becca," I said, keeping an eye on the distant curve of the driveway. "She should be pulling up soon, and we'll need to help her with the groceries."

Archer let out a low whistle. "Ah, the epitome of culinary beauty." I chuckled – and I didn't disagree with him.

Luke joined us, handing Vinnie a glass of the same scotch he was cradling. It was something of a marvel to outsiders, this bond the four of us had. We were close in a way most people found puzzling. Partners in business, best friends in life, and constant companions in whatever adventures came our way—even vacations like this one. The kinship we had was beyond words, something unspoken but deeply felt. The kinship was literal between the three brothers, though I never felt left out despite being the only non-Gallo in the group.

Yet, as grateful as I was for this brotherhood, there was still a space, an unnamed wanting that had quietly settled into a corner of my heart. It was an inarticulate yearning, not just for love, but for a shared life. A future where each of us could be our true selves, uncompromising and unafraid.

"Do you think she'll say yes?" Luke's voice broke my train of thought.

"Hmm?" I turned to look at him.

"To the proposition. For her to stay on as our personal chef even after this trip," Luke clarified. "Not just cooking for the company."

"I hope so," I found myself saying. And I did, more than I initially realized. Becca had a spark, an understated but undeniable flair—not just in the kitchen but in the way she carried herself. I found it more and more difficult to overlook.

"Too bad she works for us," Archer said, his gaze fixed on the driveway. He'd put into words something that had no doubt been on all of our minds since asking her to join us for this trip. Hell, maybe even since hiring her.

"Yeah, it is," I admitted. I had a golden rule: no dating employees. It wasn't just for the sake of appearances; it was about maintaining a balanced power dynamic. A line that shouldn't be crossed. "Gentlemen, a reminder—Becca is off-limits."

Archer grunted, savoring another sip of his wine as if it were a rare vintage. Knowing Archer, it probably was.

Vinnie appeared beside us, scotch in hand, followed by Luke.

"Isn't it a little early for the hard stuff?" I raised an eyebrow, my own cup of coffee suddenly looking quite pedestrian in comparison.

Vinnie smirked. "Isaac, we're on vacation. The usual rules don't apply."

Before I could protest, he uncorked a bottle of Bailey's Irish Cream and splashed a generous amount into my coffee. I chuckled, raising the mug to my lips. The creaminess of the Bailey's melded perfectly with the robustness of the coffee—pure indulgence, and damn if it didn't taste good.

"Not all rules are suspended," I reiterated, locking eyes with each of them in turn. I knew these men, knew them better than anyone else in the world. We had weathered storms together, celebrated victories, mourned losses. I trusted them with my life. But I also knew that men—myself included—could be fools in matters of the heart.

"I mean it. She's here to do a job. Let's not make it complicated for her or for us," I added, my tone leaving no room for negotiation. "Besides, if this works out, we could have a world-class chef taking care of our gastronomic needs on a more permanent basis. Don't screw this up."

Archer finished his wine, placing the empty glass on a small outdoor table. "So, it's business as usual, then?"

"Exactly," I said, my eyes returning to the cabin road. "Business as usual."

Her forest green Land Rover turned slowly around the bend, driving onto the main stretch of the property. Her car crunched over the gravel, stopping a short distance from where we stood. The engine cut off, and the door swung open. Becca stepped out, enveloping herself in a coat, gloves, and a beanie as though she were donning armor against the winter chill.

I couldn't peel my eyes away as she walked to the rear of her SUV, her boots imprinting on the freshly fallen snow. She lifted the trunk and glanced at the stash of groceries, then back to the four of us standing on the deck like statues on the porch.

Even in layers of winter clothing designed more for function than fashion, Becca was an undeniable knockout. Her long dark hair cascaded down her back like a waterfall at midnight, shiny and full of life, contrasting beautifully with her fair skin.

Her eyes, dark as deep pools of chocolate, were capable of holding your gaze and never letting go. Those eyes could communicate more than words ever could, full of intelligence, spunk, and a hint of mischief. But it was her curvaceous figure that caught my attention the most. Even wrapped in bulky winter attire, her body had a language all its own—curvy in all the right places, a physical testament to femininity that could make any man stop dead in his tracks.

Something stirred deep inside me, an almost primal reaction to her beauty. She radiated an aura of sensual allure yet maintained an air of graceful sophistication. It was a tantalizing mix, and I felt a surge of desire so potent it took me by surprise. My pulse quickened, and for a moment, the snowy landscape, the cabin, and even my life-long friends faded into the background, leaving only her.

"Are you gentlemen just going to stand there and watch me carry in all these groceries by myslelf?"

The air seemed to burst with her humor, and we all chuckled. I glanced at the guys, each of us sharing the same appreciative look, then marched down the steps toward her.

"As it turns out, I'm a part-time grocery-hauling super-hero," I said, grabbing a couple of bags and leading the way back to the cabin. Vinnie, Luke, and Archer followed suit, each grabbing an armful of groceries.

As we unloaded the supplies into the cabin's entryway so we could take off our coats, I caught myself watching Becca again. She moved with grace and a surefooted ease, already at home in our mountain retreat. Something about her felt both new and wonderfully familiar, like a song you've never heard before but already know the words to.

Could we really maintain a purely professional distance? The thought buzzed in my head like a persistent fly. We had our rules, built over years of friendship and business partnership. But rules are man-made, and men are fallible creatures.

What made this especially complex was our unique relationship; the four of us had shared before—though now wasn't the time to delve into that. The point was, we understood the tenuous nature of desire, how easily boundaries could blur when emotions came into play.

As we finalized the placement of the last bag, Becca clapped her gloved hands together.

"Alright, let's make some culinary magic happen!" she declared, already taking charge of her dominion.

I felt both excitement and a twinge of apprehension. This trip was either going to be a spectacular success or a recipe for disaster. And looking at the other faces in the room—Vinnie with his devil-may-care grin, Archer's eyes piercing as if he were solving a complex algorithm, and Luke, the watchful observer—I knew they were grappling with the same possibilities.

The stakes were different this time; the game had changed. We were all smart enough to know that when you introduce a new variable into a stable equation, the outcomes can be unpredictable. The question was, were we prepared for whatever solution that new variable might yield?

Only time would tell. But damn, if the game itself didn't suddenly seem a lot more interesting.

CHAPTER 3

BECCA

As I walked further into the cabin, my eyes instantly found them again—Isaac, Archer, Luke, and Vinnie—standing like four gods. My breath hitched involuntarily. Each one was a masterpiece of testosterone and muscle, exuding effortless charm only a man confident in his own skin could radiate. For a split second, I wondered how on Earth I was going to spend five days there without turning into a walking hormone.

As I slipped out of my coat, I mentally shook off the inappropriate thoughts, reminding myself that I was there for a job. All the same, there was no escaping the electrifying energy pulsating in the air.

As I walked closer, they surrounded me, and suddenly I was enveloped in a heady aroma that was part pine, part masculine spice, and all intoxicating. My senses were overwhelmed; it was as if every nerve ending in my body was standing at attention, hyper-aware of their proximity.

To cope, I fell back on my go-to defense mechanism—humor. "Good Lord, did you guys roll around in a pine forest before I arrived?" I waved my hand theatrically in front of my face. "I'm gonna need to dig out my allergy meds if you keep this up."

They all chuckled, finding my sarcasm endearing, or maybe they were just being polite. But their laughter did nothing to dispel the electric current in the air. If anything, it seemed to amplify it. The men shucked off their coats, Archer coming over to me, deftly plucking mine out of my hands and hanging it up nearby.

Isaac's eyes met mine, and for a moment, everything else faded away. His gaze held an intensity that was almost predatory, like a wolf eyeing its prey. My heart pounded in my chest so loudly I was convinced they could all hear it.

Vinnie took a step closer, and I caught a whiff of his cologne, something woodsy and expensive. My pulse spiked, a reaction that was entirely too visceral to ignore.

Luke shot me a smile that, despite its subtlety, sent a jolt down my spine. It was as though he knew something I didn't, a secret that was both thrilling and a bit terrifying.

And then there was Archer, covered in tattoos but as poised as a statue. His gaze was more blatant, brazen even, as it traveled over me. He seemed like a man who took what he wanted, consequences be damned. His intense stare sent a shiver through my body.

All of this happened within a span of seconds, but it was enough to throw my equilibrium completely off balance. Hormones, professionalism, and undeniable sexual tension blended together in a chaotic mix, leaving me disoriented yet oddly exhilarated.

Five days, I reminded myself. I just have to get through five days. But as their eyes continued to bore into me, each offering a different kind of danger and allure, I couldn't help but wonder—did I even stand a chance?

"Wow, you must drive like our nona if you're only just

getting here," Vinnie teased, his eyes twinkling with mischief.

I laughed. "Well, I had to make sure I arrived in one piece. Who else would cook for you big, helpless men?"

Luke joined in, "Helpless is a strong word, Chef. I mean, we can boil water and even make instant ramen. Gourmet stuff."

I rolled my eyes playfully and dramatically. "Oh, the culinary prowess! I'm clearly outmatched."

As Archer, Luke, and Isaac moved to collect the groceries, Vinnie did something entirely unexpected. He reached out and took my hand, leading me to the living room. His hand was warm, strong, and so large it almost engulfed mine. The contact was simple but electric, sending a surge of something intense and heady straight to my core. I could feel my pulse quicken, and I became hyper-aware of the sensation of his skin against mine.

Once inside the room, any thoughts of Vinnie's hand—or any other part of him—were temporarily erased by sheer awe. I was standing in a space that could only be described as the epitome of luxury. My mouth dropped open, but words escaped me.

Vinnie seemed to enjoy my flabbergasted reaction, a smug grin forming on his lips. "You like the view?"

"This place is like a palace," I managed to stammer.

His laughter filled the room, a rich, hearty sound that made the atmosphere seem lighter, cozier. "Well, we like to be comfortable."

Comfortable was an understatement. I was still taking in the sheer grandeur of the place when Vinnie led me through the living room and into the kitchen. Again, I was blown away. State-of-the-art appliances, marble counter-tops, a stove that looked like it could handle a Thanksgiving feast for forty. This was not just any kitchen; it was a chef's fantasy.

"I hope this suits you," Vinnie said as I took in the sight of the splendor before me.

"Are you kidding? This is a *dream*."

As Vinnie showed me around, pointing out where I could find various pots, pans, and utensils, I tried to focus on his words, but it was difficult. The feeling of his hand in mine had not left me, and I was uncomfortably aware of how close he was standing. Every so often, he would lean in to open a cupboard or point out a feature, and I could feel the heat emanating from him, enveloping me in that intoxicating blend of pine and masculinity.

When our tour finally ended, I realized my cheeks were flushed, my breath shallow. How was I supposed to survive five days with these four impossibly attractive men?

"Come on," he said once we were done in the kitchen. "Let me show you the rest of the place."

Three stories tall, the building seemed to blend effortlessly with the surrounding woodland, its Swiss-style architecture giving off an air of understated luxury.

The entrance foyer alone was more spacious than my entire apartment, decked out in plush rugs and polished wood flooring that extended into the living room. The centerpiece was a monumental stone fireplace, reaching almost to the ceiling, adorned with intricate carvings and flanked by oversized leather armchairs that looked like they'd swallow you whole in comfort.

And oh, the living room. It was like something out of a magazine—a perfect balance of opulence and coziness. The furnishings were obviously high-end, from the velvet-upholstered couches to the antique coffee table that looked like it belonged in a museum. Yet, for all its luxury, the room still felt inviting. Large windows stretched from floor to ceiling, providing panoramic views of the snow-covered mountains outside. Fluffy throws were carelessly draped over the back of the couches, and I could imagine curling up here, hot chocolate in hand, as the snow fell outside.

As Vinnie continued the tour, my jaw practically hit the floor more than once. The dining room was equally grand, with a table long enough to seat at least twelve and a chandelier that would have looked at home in a castle. Then there were the bedrooms—each more luxurious than the last, all ensuite, complete with deep-soak tubs and rainfall showers.

On the top floor, Vinnie showed me a home theater with cinema-style seating and a popcorn machine in the corner. And then he opened the door to a private library—walls lined with books from floor to ceiling, a telescope positioned by the window for stargazing, and a writing desk that looked out over the sprawling mountains.

"And there's a gym in the basement," he said. "Well, to be more accurate, the gym *is* the basement. Feel free to use it whenever you want."

As we circled back to the living room, I felt a mix of awe and disbelief. This cabin was more than just a luxurious retreat; it was a wonderland, carefully balancing grandiosity with the kind of coziness that made you want to stay forever. It was, in a word, perfection. And I was about to spend the next five days here.

"This place is something else," I said.

He chuckled. "We might've gone a little overboard when we planned it. But hey, life in the city has a way of making you crave a retreat like this. Come on – I'll show you your bedroom."

Vinnie led me to a room that forced me to pause in the

doorway to absorb the sheer beauty of it. The large windows offered a breathtaking view of the snow-covered mountains, almost like a painting hung for my personal enjoyment. The room itself was a masterpiece—plush carpeting, an opulent bed adorned with silk linens, and elegant furnishings that somehow still felt cozy.

"You might want to close those curtains," Vinnie said, pointing toward the window. "The sun rises right there. Unless you want a five am wake-up call from Mother Nature herself."

I chuckled. "I'll be in the kitchen every day by six to make breakfast, so that won't be an issue."

He looked surprised. "That's really not necessary. You can sleep in if you want."

"Oh, I know both you and Isaac are early risers. I am too, so it's no big deal. Plus, I'm being paid to make sure food is ready when you guys are hungry."

Just as I was inspecting the closet space, Luke and Archer walked in, carrying my luggage like it weighed nothing.

"Where would you like these?" Luke asked.

"Just on the bed is fine, thanks." Once they had set down my bags, I turned to them. "Thank you so much for bringing my stuff up. If it's alright with you, I'll unpack and then head down to the kitchen."

"Of course," Archer said.

Vinnie strode to the doorway and turned to look at me. "If you need anything, don't hesitate to ask."

The way he said it sent a tingling sensation down my spine, triggering another wave of hormones I absolutely did not need right now. I laughed to defuse my growing tension. "Unless you can chop vegetables or baste a turkey, I think I'll manage."

Archer's lips curved into a sly smile. "Well, if you ever want to teach me, I'm a quick learner."

"Yeah, a real master baster, you could say," Vinnie added, wearing a smirk of his own.

Archer laughed. "Shithead."

With that, I was alone. I sat on the edge of the bed, taking in the sight of the gorgeous room and equally beautiful view. How the hell was I going to go back to my shoe-drawer-sized Chinatown apartment after spending nearly a week in this place?

As nice as the bedroom was, however, I couldn't resist the call of the kitchen, bounding off the bed and heading downstairs. Once there, I had to stop and take a moment to just breathe. It was like something out of my wildest dreams. From the gleaming stainless-steel appliances to the perfectly organized spice racks and the vast marble countertops, the space screamed luxury and efficiency. I circled around, opening various drawers and cabinets, each filled with top-of-the-line utensils and gadgets. The guys were there, plucking drinks out of the fridge and snacking on odds and ends.

"You guys better be careful," I warned them, my eyes not leaving the stove.

Archer raised an eyebrow. "What do you mean?"

"This kitchen makes our work kitchen look like a hot plate in a college dorm. You realize I'm going to be asking for upgrades now, right?"

Isaac chuckled, leaning against the counter, the corner of his mouth curling into a hint of a smile. "Well, if the meals you prepare this week are as spectacular as they usually are, who knows? We might have to consider some upgrades."

I grinned, locking eyes with him. "Challenge accepted.

And no snacking – I want you all good and hungry for dinner."

"Yes, ma'am," Vinnie replied with a grin.

I left them standing there, trying not to appear as giddy as I felt. I climbed the stairs back to my room, my thoughts a confusing whirlwind. As I began to unpack, laying out my clothes and arranging my toiletries, the professional in me took over. I had a job to do, and whether in a dorm-like kitchen or a gourmet one, I was going to knock their socks off.

L uke let out a long whistle through his teeth as soon as Becca was out of earshot.

"That ass though," he commented, a cheeky grin on his face.

Archer grunted in agreement, his eyes still following her as she disappeared around the corner. I shook my head at both of them.

"Gentlemen, as the voice of reason here—and also as the one who doesn't want to get sued—let me remind you, she's off limits." I leaned back against the kitchen counter as I spoke.

Isaac seconded it. "Vinnie's right. Off limits, guys." However, I could sense that he was a little disappointed by the idea of not flirting with Becca, even a little.

Archer, as if drawn by a magnet, started wandering toward the kitchen. "Sure, sure," he said, "but someone's got to make sure she's settling in okay."

Luke suddenly stood up, eyeing his twin. "Well, if we're going that way, I need more scotch."

As they sauntered off, no doubt finding an excuse to be

in close proximity to our delectable new chef, I turned to Isaac. "You think bringing her here might've been a bad idea?"

Isaac took a sip of his Bailey's-infused coffee, shrugging his broad shoulders. "We're all adults, Vinnie. We have the ability to control our libidos."

I let out a laugh, unable to keep a straight face. "Oh, come on, Mr. Self-Control. I saw you staring at her ass just as much as Luke was."

Isaac raised an eyebrow, clearly caught. But he maintained that steady, unflappable demeanor that had served him well in board meetings and negotiations. "Observing and acting are two different things," he retorted, taking a slow sip.

"Observing, huh? Is that what we're calling it these days?"

He chuckled, setting his mug down on the table beside him. "Look, Vin, she's a professional, we're professionals. We hired her to cook, not to become the center of some romantic drama."

I nodded, partly convinced. "Alright, but if Archer starts trying to impress her by dismantling kitchen appliances, or Luke offers to be her taste-tester, we're intervening."

Isaac smiled, the kind of smile that was all knowing and a bit ominous. "Agreed. But for now, let's give everyone the benefit of the doubt."

Easy for him to say, but as the buffer between his gruffer personality and our clients, I could definitely foresee potential complications. Isaac might have trusted us to be adults, but history had shown that adulting was not exactly our strong suit when a beautiful woman was involved.

"Okay, the woman is a looker. No doubt about that. But

we manage to control ourselves in a professional setting at work; we can do the same here."

"I don't know," I reply, my tone laced with pragmatic caution. "Vacation is basically the Bermuda Triangle of good decisions. It's where rules go to die."

Isaac didn't say anything to that, but the sudden peal of Becca's laughter from the kitchen acted like a siren's call. As if on cue, we both veered toward the kitchen, our steps syncing up like soldiers marching to a different kind of battle.

When we walked in, Luke and Archer were sitting at the kitchen island, their gazes fixed on Becca as if she was the eighth wonder of the world. She was busy arranging the groceries in the cupboards, giving out orders like a seasoned general.

"No, no, don't help me. I like things where I like them," she said, flashing them a smile somehow both firm and inviting.

My eyes followed her as she moved around the kitchen, and my cock stiffened when she stretched to reach a higher shelf. Her shirt lifted just a bit, exposing a tantalizing slice of skin. I found myself agreeing with Luke's earlier appraisal. That ass in those jeans? God help us all.

I snapped back to reality, locking eyes with Isaac for a moment. We shared a knowing look, a silent agreement being made. Yes, she was attractive—distractingly so—but we were here for a break, not to complicate our lives. Easier said than done, of course, especially when the woman in question seemed capable of breaking down more than just culinary barriers.

Archer rose gracefully from his seat, gesturing toward the glass of meticulously chosen wine he'd been nursing. "You sure you don't want some? It's a good year."

"I don't drink while I'm cooking," she said, punctuating her refusal with a smile. "Only after. Will you guys be ready for dinner in about an hour?"

We all nodded in agreement.

She continued, laying out her culinary schedule with the authority of a five-star general. "I've got breakfast covered by seven, but if any of you want to sleep in, it'll be kept warm. Lunch is at 12:30 sharp. Dinner is a seven pm affair unless you've got different plans."

Her precision caught me off guard, and I couldn't help but voice my appreciation. "Works great for me – nice and regimented."

She grinned, taking the compliment in stride. "Someone's got to keep you guys in line."

"Speaking of which, how about a snack? I could eat a horse," I quipped, throwing a playful glance her way.

She rolled her eyes but laughed, "Oh my God, you're like a five-year-old. Sit tight."

In what felt like mere seconds, an array of cheeses, meats, and crackers took form on a cutting board. Not only did it look delicious, it looked like art. Everything was arranged perfectly. Jesus, she was like a culinary ninja.

Isaac, our ever-responsible leader, nudged us toward the door. "Let's move this to the living room. Give Chef the space she needs to work her magic."

Her eyes twinkled as she waved us away. "You heard the man. Get outta my kitchen."

I felt a strange sense of loss as we walked away. Isaac picked up the charcuterie board, leading the way. Archer and Luke followed, but I could tell they were as reluctant as I was to leave her magnetic pull. There was something about Becca's energy. Her laugh had notes that reached inside you, coaxing out a response. You wanted to stay, to listen, to be in her aura a little longer.

I tossed her one last question the way out. "Do you need a sous chef? I can slice and dice with the best of them," I asked, a half-smile playing on my lips.

She chuckled warmly, and the sound felt like sunlight cutting through fog. "Nope, I've got it. Now go, shoo! Enjoy your vacation, some of us have to work."

Her dismissal was softened by her humor, and I found myself grinning as I rejoined the others. Yet as I took a step away, I risked one final glance back at her. It was like seeing her for the first time. She had been right under our noses, serving meals day in and day out at the office for the whole C-suite, and now I felt like I had been blind.

She was captivating—her movements, the animated way she talked, the confident sway of her hips; they all painted a picture of a woman who was beautiful, spunky, and incredibly alluring. And for the first time, it dawned on me how unprepared I was for the emotional complexity she added to what was supposed to be a straightforward trip.

The potential of the next five days stretched out in my mind like a maze filled with dangerous curves and bewitching laughter. A maze that smelled suspiciously like the best meals I'd ever had and sounded like a symphony of flirtatious banter and clinking glasses.

A maze that, for all my skill in navigating people and situations, left me utterly disoriented.

Isaac might think we're all adults, capable of handling our emotions, our attractions. But as I sat back on the plush couch, my eyes drifting to the kitchen where she was undoubtedly weaving culinary spells, I couldn't help but think that some mazes were designed to get you lost.

And man, what a beautiful way to be lost.

CHAPTER 5

LUKE

Perched on the deck, I held a glass of smokey scotch in my hand, its burn grounding me as I lost myself in thought. The snow-covered landscape stretched out before me, still and quiet. The solitude brought clarity. I'd always found it easier to think when I was alone.

Becca. She had been on my mind since the moment she pulled up, her smile shining brighter than the afternoon sun reflecting off the snow. But even before that, she was a constant presence—always there in the peripheral, her energy adding life to the mundane daily grind of office work.

I had noticed her from the beginning; it was hard not to. She had this innate charm, this vitality that drew you in. She was also stunning.

I also noticed something else—how my brothers and Isaac seemed blissfully ignorant of her allure. At least, that's how it appeared. The "no dating employees" rule Isaac implemented had made it easier to ignore the tug of attraction. The rule served as a convenient barrier, something to hide behind.

But as I observed the unfolding scene in the kitchen, the unspoken electricity in the air became undeniable. The way Archer offered her that glass of wine, his eyes lingering just a second too long. Vinnie, ever the charmer, looking at her as if she were the sunrise, unique and awe-inspiring. And Isaac, ever so stoic and reserved, gravitating toward her as if pulled by some invisible force.

Each gesture was small but telling, and the sum of it all pointed to a truth none of us wanted to admit: Becca was a magnetic field, and we were but iron filings, helpless in our attraction.

In my gut, I knew bringing her here might complicate things. A workplace crush was one thing; it lived and died by the strictures of professional decorum. But a vacation was a setting of intimacy, of letting your guard down. The boundaries could blur. Rules, especially unspoken ones, were more likely to break under the weight of proximity and shared moments.

I took another sip of my scotch, letting the liquid courage bolster me. Our unspoken pact of non-interference with Becca might hold within the walls of FourSquare, but there, amidst nature's beauty and isolation, all bets were off.

Isaac said we were all adults, capable of controlling our desires, but the truth was, attraction wasn't something you could control. It was a wildfire—unpredictable, all-consuming. You might be able to contain it, manage it for a while, but under the right conditions, it would break free and roar to life, sweeping away all your carefully constructed boundaries.

I gazed at the mountains in the distance, wondering what the next few days would hold. There was an untamed beauty in their peaks and valleys, something raw and uncompromising. They stood as a testament to the unpredictability of nature. Just like the woman who had entered our lives, altering the topography in ways we had yet to fully understand.

Savoring another sip of scotch, my thoughts swirled around Becca. The way her laughter filled the kitchen earlier, light and melodic. The curve of her smile, the sparkle in her eyes. I was not blind to the energy between us, and I was also aware she was intelligent enough to pick up on it too. Yet something told me she was not one to cross lines, especially not professional ones. Her integrity appeared to be as real as her beauty, and that was saying something.

We prided ourselves on integrity as well. It was part of the foundational ethics Isaac had instilled in the business. But this—this was different. Becca posed a challenge, a test of our unspoken pact. I grinned into my glass at the thought. Things were about to get complicated, and I'd be lying if I said I didn't find that exciting.

My ears caught the sound of the sliding door opening behind me, snapping me out of my musings. I turned to see Archer stepping out onto the deck, a glass of red wine in hand. He grunted, a monosyllabic articulation that spoke volumes. The beauty of being a twin was that words were often unnecessary.

"Feeling like a love-struck teenager on your first date?" I chuckled, my words tinged with both jest and empathy.

Archer shot me a look that clearly said he didn't appreciate my attempt at humor, but his eyes couldn't hide what I already knew to be true—he was as enthralled by her as I was.

"You feel it too, huh?" Archer finally broke his silence, leaning against the railing next to me.

"It's hard not to."

"Vinnie's smitten. Even Isaac, Mr. 'No Fraternization,' can't seem to keep his eyes off her," Archer added.

"Yeah," I agreed, allowing the weight of the revelation to settle. "You remember that time in LA? The actress?"

Archer's eyes met mine, clearly recalling the shared escapade, a tantalizing past experience that shattered our collective self-restraint. Four men, one beautiful woman. The memory hung in the air between us, a cautionary tale of what could happen when rules were thrown to the wind.

"Think history's about to repeat itself?" Archer finally asked, pulling me from the labyrinth of my thoughts.

I pondered the question, swirling the scotch at the bottom of my glass. The truth was, I didn't know. What I did know was that Becca wasn't just a temptation; she was a red line, a challenge to the professional and personal boundaries we'd all set. And like it or not, we were standing dangerously close to it.

"I guess we'll find out," I said, taking a final gulp of my scotch and setting the glass aside. I met Archer's gaze, both of us aware that we were standing on the precipice of something fraught with peril, yet undeniably exhilarating.

And just like that, the gauntlet had been thrown, the die cast. We all felt it, the gravitational pull of desire drawing us ever closer to a point of no return.

"Now you've got me thinking about Jessica," Archer's words shattered the silence, naming the actress who had briefly tangled our lives in LA. "Feels like déjà vu, doesn't it?"

The memories from that escapade washed over me. Things with Jessica had gone a bit sideways, but the fault had not been ours. It had been fun while it lasted though.

"Do you think Isaac and Vinnie might be open to, well, exploring a bit?"

Archer laughed, a rich, throaty sound that reflected both amusement and contemplation. "Did you see how they were looking at her? I think the question is moot."

A momentary silence settled between us, the night alive with the distant rustle of trees and the whisper of the wind. We were both wrestling with the same quandary.

"You know," Archer finally said, "the only way we're going to know if she's even interested is to let things happen naturally. Asking her directly could be playing with fire. Worst-case scenario, it's harassment and grounds for a lawsuit."

"I agree. If something's going to happen, it'll happen naturally, organically. There's no pushing it," I added. "At the end of the day, it's her choice. We can feel whatever we feel, but she's the one who'd have to be interested in navigating these waters with us."

"And I'd say we're all on the same page about her," Archer concluded, locking eyes with me. His gaze was an echo of my own thoughts.

We were all adults, all capable of making our choices. Yet as I stood there, staring at the mountains bathed in moonlight, I couldn't help but wonder about the choices that awaited us in the coming days.

The air was thick with uncertainty and unspoken desires, but one thing was clear: Becca wasn't just another woman, and this wasn't just another vacation.

The next five days were going to be a journey, not just through the snow-covered trails outside, but through the labyrinth of emotions, desires, and decisions that awaited us.

CHAPTER 6

ISAAC

Sitting at the desk in the makeshift office I'd set up for this supposed "vacation," I found myself unable to focus. I'd read through the same quarterly marketing report three times, and it might as well have been in a foreign language for all the sense it was making. Normally, it would be child's play for me.

With Becca occupying ninety percent of my brain, however, things were a different story.

Closing my eyes momentarily, I tried to clear my head, to bring my focus back to the numbers, the projections, the targets. But all that came to mind was Becca—her eyes, the curve of her lips, the lilt in her laughter. She was stunning, not just visually but in her totality. Smart, sharp-witted, and discerning—she made her point without being mean, her jokes somehow managing to include rather than alienate.

She had something—the kind of aura that made you want to be better just by being around her. She had it in spades, but the problem was, she reminded me of Mindy. Mindy, the woman who once filled my thoughts just like Becca was doing now, the woman who took my heart and trampled it into a thousand pieces. The thought made my jaw tighten involuntarily. Becca, however, was a universe apart from Mindy in one key area: she didn't seem to have a cruel bone in her body.

I shook my head, ridding myself of the ghost of relationships past. Comparing her to Mindy didn't do Becca justice. She was her own person, deserving of being seen for who she was, not as a reflection of someone else.

Leaning back in the chair, I let out a frustrated sigh. What the hell was I doing cooped up in this office wrestling with memories and what-ifs when the living, breathing inspiration for all this mental turmoil was mere steps away? And why did the thought of her affect me so much? I'd always been good at keeping my personal and professional life separate. This blurring of boundaries wasn't like me.

I swirled the scotch in my glass, my eyes darting back to the damned marketing report. For the third time, the words blurred into a meaningless jumble. My mind was already miles away—specifically, just downstairs in the kitchen.

I imagined bumping into Becca in the kitchen late at night, both of us unable to sleep. Maybe she'd be whipping up some late-night dessert, the room filled with the warm scent of cinnamon and sugar. In my fantasy, I found myself leaning against the kitchen counter, just watching her, captivated. Our eyes would meet, and we'd share a knowing smile.

Each step closer would feel like a magnetic pull, our eyes locked, saying what words couldn't. Finally, I'd close the gap, our lips meeting in a kiss that would start off as soft but would quickly deepen—a mix of urgency and exploration. My hands would find the curve of her waist, pulling her closer, while hers would journey up my arms, her fingers lightly grazing the nape of my neck.

The tension would escalate, each touch setting off sparks that had been simmering ever since we first laid eyes on each other. And just as I imagined her hand drifting lower, inching toward--

"Get a grip," I muttered to myself, snapping out of the tantalizing daydream. I forced my eyes back to the marketing report, that damned anchor to reality.

My eyes fell on the leather-bound notebook beside my laptop, filled with years of hard-earned business wisdom. As if pulled by an invisible force, my hand picked it up, flipped it opened to a random page.

"Total control is an illusion," read the handwritten note, a lesson I learned the hard way years ago.

Maybe that was just it. Maybe I couldn't control how Becca made me feel, any more than I could control the tides or the phases of the moon. For the first time in a long time, I allowed myself to consider the possibility of something outside the realm of spreadsheets and five-year plans.

However, what I *could* control were my actions. I could let my attraction to Becca stay locked away in my mind, the secret never to escape.

Taking a deep breath, I reached for the glass of scotch Vinnie had poured earlier, relishing the smooth burn as it glided down my throat. The rich, oaky flavors settled in, and for a moment, my mind cleared.

Focus, I reminded myself, focus.

Work didn't pause just because I decided to take a break, a reality I accepted long ago. FourSight wasn't just a business; it was my life's work, my brainchild. Luke, Archer, Vinnie, and I had built it into a billion-dollar enterprise, but that sort of success didn't maintain itself. One doesn't get to the top by accident, and staying there required a constant, vigilant effort.

Vacation or not, I'd committed to spending a chunk of each day handling work affairs. Calls, emails, reviewing reports like the damn marketing one I can't seem to get past today—all part of the grind. After all, the empire wouldn't run itself, and neither would the various departments we each headed.

I set the glass down, its weight echoing my thoughts. There was a sense of responsibility that came with being at the helm of a company like FourSight. It was like a child that needed to be nurtured and guarded. And just as a parent would never completely neglect their child, even for a holiday, I couldn't fully step away from the company.

I gazed at the report again, forcing my eyes to process the graphs, the numbers, the bullet points. This time, they began making sense, aligning themselves into the coherent analysis they were meant to be. Satisfied, I started making notes, mentally strategizing the next quarter's approach.

As my pen danced across the paper, a fragment of laughter pierced through the closed door—a light, melodious sound that, for a second, made me pause and look up. Becca. The momentary distraction didn't last long, but it was enough, enough to remind me that while my commitment to my business was unyielding, life had its own plans, its own distractions, its own unpredictability. And as much as I'd like to think otherwise, maybe that wasn't such a bad thing.

Consciously, I returned to the report, but in the back of my mind, a small compartment opened, reserved for the possibility of something new, something unexpected. As I immersed myself into the world of market trends and revenue streams, it was this small, untouched compartment that kept me grounded, that kept me human. And in a life dictated by figures and bottom lines, that small fragment of potential seemed more valuable than ever.

The door creaked open, and before I even looked up, a waft of some heavenly aroma filled the room. It was Becca, standing at the threshold, looking as if she had just walked out of a culinary magazine. "Dinner's about ready," she announced softly.

She paused, her eyes meeting mine, a puzzled expression shaping her face. "What's up? You look like you've got other things on your mind than food."

If only she knew.

"Working," I replied curtly, not willing to admit the focus I usually had in spades seemed to be diluted today.

She took a few steps closer, her footfalls softly thudding against the hardwood floor, and the scent of whatever culinary magic she had cooked enveloping her, enveloping the room. "You do know you're on vacation, right?"

A sardonic laugh escaped my lips. "Vacation is a state of mind, Becca, one that most CEOs can't afford."

She walked up to the desk, placing her hands on her hips, and I swear my heart missed a beat. "Isaac, I see you at work, you know. You're usually there long after I've served dinner. You're always the last to leave, hunched over your desk like some sort of workaholic hermit."

For a moment, I was caught off guard. Her keen observation wrapped in a light, teasing tone sliced through the self-imposed boundary I had built around myself. The boundary that allowed me to live a life of numbers, graphs, and never-ending emails.

"Yeah, well, you don't build a billion-dollar company by clocking out at five," I retorted, although her words had already found their mark, pricking at the bubble of invulnerability I liked to think I had built.

"I get that," she said, her voice softening. "But Isaac, even CEOs need to eat. And relax. And maybe even enjoy a week away from the grind."

I looked into her eyes, and for a moment, I saw an understanding, a depth that went beyond the simple mechanics of employer and employee. It was unsettling and comforting at the same time, a contradiction I couldn't quite reconcile.

Sighing, I closed the laptop, suddenly aware of how ridiculous it was to be locked up in a room while surrounded by the beauty of nature, the promise of good food, and the company of people who, whether I liked it or not, made my life richer.

"Alright, Chef," I said, standing up. "Let's go see what you've whipped up."

As we walked out of the room, I felt a strange sense of liberation. Maybe it was the mountains, maybe it was the break from routine, or maybe it was just Becca's candid words. Whatever it was, for the first time in a long while, the weight of my responsibilities felt a little lighter.

As we left the office, my footsteps fell in sync with Becca's, filling the space with an audible, rhythmic tension. It felt like the prelude to something unspoken, a gathering storm of words and possibilities neither of us could entirely articulate.

"You're really familiar with my habits, aren't you?" I finally said, breaking the silence but not the tension that had been steadily mounting between us.

"I know you stay up all hours of the night, practically live on that leather couch in your office, and use the executive bathroom to look somewhat human in the morning," she replied, a hint of concern tinging her voice. "Isaac, it's not healthy. No matter how much responsibility you carry, you need to take breaks. Otherwise, you'll break down, and what good will that do anyone, including you?"

Her words hit me like a shot of scotch—sharp, warm, and unexpectedly soothing. And it genuinely surprised me how much she seemed to care. "You're concerned about my health?" I asked, trying to mask the confusion and wonderment starting to well up inside me.

She stopped, turned to look at me, and smiled—a smile that was part empathy, part mystery. "Someone has to tell you these things, Isaac, or you're going to work yourself into an early grave. Or a heart attack."

I was struck by the sincerity in her voice, the genuine concern that seemed to emanate from her. It was a vulnerability I had carefully avoided in my professional life, a soft spot I had consciously hardened to maintain the tough-as-nails persona that had become my corporate hallmark. Yet, here, in this moment, with her, it all seemed to come undone.

"Thanks for caring, Becca," I said, my voice softer than I had intended, my shield of emotional armor feeling a little less secure. "I'm not used to people worrying about me. Especially not someone who works for me."

Her eyes met mine, and I could see something there—something that made me think she was not just another employee, not just another face in the crowd. "Well, maybe it's time to get used to it," she replied. "And maybe it's time to start taking better care of yourself. Starting with a good meal."

CHAPTER 7

BECCA

I poured him a glass of wine—nothing too fancy, just a vintage that would pair well with the night's culinary adventure.

"Here," I said, handing him the glass, "to whet your appetite."

Isaac took a sip, looking every bit the CEO even in his casual vacation attire. "This smells amazing, Becca. What is it?"

A playful grin crept onto my face. "Ah, patience, Mr. CEO. That's a virtue, you know. Just know that Archer's not the only wine expert here now."

He rolled his eyes, but the grin on his face told me he was intrigued, maybe even a bit charmed. "It's a need-to-know basis, huh?"

"Exactly," I quipped, turning my attention to the sizzling pan in front of me.

The moment I was face to face with my sautéing garlic and herbs, my internal critic piped up. *What the hell, Becca? This is your boss, not your college roommate.* But despite the loud clanging of 'employee etiquette' alarms in my head, talking to Isaac felt...well, it felt normal. Easy, even. Our difference in standing seemed to dissolve the moment I stepped into the kitchen, transforming from his personal chef into some strange hybrid of culinary artist and candid confidante.

I flipped a medley of veggies in the pan, their vibrant colors a stark contrast to the mundane numbers and reports Isaac always buried his nose in. I loved that contrast—the uncomplicated joy of cooking versus the convoluted world of business he navigated daily. For a moment, I imagined Isaac leaving behind his sea of endless spreadsheets and emails and diving into my world of flavors, spices, and textures. A world where, believe it or not, a perfectly balanced dish could solve more problems than a quarterly report.

As I plated the food—carefully arranging it into what I liked to think of as an edible masterpiece—I couldn't help but consider the layers of Isaac I'd started to uncover. Beyond the rigid exterior of a relentless businessman was a man who could appreciate a good meal, a good wine, and maybe even good company that wasn't listed on the Fortune 500.

I glanced at him. He was fidgeting with his phone, prob-ably negotiating a million-dollar deal or something equally intimidating. Yet there he was, in my kitchen, waiting to taste my food. And in that moment, the boundaries between employer and employee felt irrelevant, replaced by a more human connection we were just beginning to explore.

"You know, if it wasn't for your cooking, I'd probably live on a diet of Joe's Pizza, Shake Shack, and Mamouns Falafel while vegetating at my desk."

I laughed, picturing the quintessential New York

takeout spread cluttering his immaculate office. "Oh, so you'd basically be a Wall Street bro?"

"Something like that," he grinned, glass of wine in hand.

My eyes flitted over him—crisp, white shirt tucked into well-fitted jeans—a far cry from any frat boy or a 24/7 office dweller. Before I knew what was happening, the words just tumbled out. "Though you obviously have time to work out."

Oh God. My face instantly flushed fifty shades of 'I-can't-believe-I-just-said-that.' I turned back to the stove as if a sudden interest in the simmering sauce could rewind the last ten seconds.

He set his napkin on the table and stood up. With wine glass in hand, he started walking toward me. My stomach knotted. This was it. He was finally going to call me out on being too...too whatever I was being.

"You think I look like I work out?" he said, stopping just a few feet from me. His tone was unreadable, and I dared not turn around to gauge his expression.

I gripped the spatula like a lifeline. "I mean, you don't look like someone who survives on falafel and burgers, that's for sure."

He laughed, a genuine, hearty laugh that echoed through the kitchen, and I felt the tension in my shoulders ease. Maybe I hadn't crossed a line; maybe I'd accidentally stumbled upon a new one—a line neither of us had expected to find but now held all the promise of uncharted territory.

I straightened, still flustered but also somewhat emboldened by the wine and the genuine nature of our conversation. "Look, I'm sorry if I overstepped. I'll leave you to—"

Before I could finish, Isaac reached out and took my hand, stopping me in my tracks. My eyes dropped to our interlocked hands. His was large, engulfing mine, his fingers strong and secure. I was surprised, yet it felt undeniably natural.

When I looked up, he was staring into my eyes with an intensity I had only ever seen directed at quarterly reports and business strategies. "Becca, I'm not used to anyone caring about my health, my well-being outside of a professional context. So, I just wanted to thank you."

The words hung in the air, almost tangible, like you could reach out and touch them. "You're welcome, Isaac," I said softly, smiling. My hand was still in his, and neither of us seemed to be in a hurry to change that. "So," I ventured, "are you going to try and stop working so much this week? You are on vacation, after all."

He seemed to ponder this for a moment before answering. "I'll try."

And then he smiled. Not a polite, business-meeting smile, but an actual, honest-to-God, reaches-the-eyes smile. It was brilliant, and from what I'd seen in my time working for him, exceedingly rare. I felt honored, a little like a birdwatcher who'd just spotted an elusive species.

Caught in the moment, caught in that smile, I felt myself leaning toward him, almost involuntarily. My lips parted, my eyes met his, and for a few heart-stopping seconds, it seemed like he was considering leaning down those extra inches to close the gap between us, to do what I suddenly realized I very much wanted him to do.

My heart pounded in my chest, its rhythm drowning out all the other sounds—the simmer of the sauce on the stove, the distant chatter of other people in the house, the rational part of my brain telling me I was playing with fire. But right now, all I wanted was to get burned. And by the look in his eyes, by the way his gaze flicked down to my lips and then back up to my eyes, it seemed like maybe he did too.

Just when I thought the universe might actually be conspiring in my favor for once, a loud bang echoed from the living room. It jolted me back to reality, like a cold splash of water on a sleepy face. I stepped back, pulling my hand from his, and immediately felt an inexplicable sense of loss. But I couldn't let that show, not when my boss and I had just tiptoed to the edge of something professionally dangerous.

"Sounds like the Gallos are up to no good. You've got five minutes to get to the dinner table," I said, winking cheekily to defuse the thick tension still lingering in the air.

That damned smile was back, causing my knees to feel like they were made of something far less solid than bone. "I'll be there," he promised.

"See that you are," I shot back, attempting nonchalance but suspecting I was fooling no one, least of all myself.

As I turned back to the meal I was preparing, my heart was racing and my thoughts were a scrambled mess. How in the name of Julia Child was I supposed to maintain any semblance of professionalism when my boss looked like that, smiled like that, and held my hand like that?

As if that weren't enough to disrupt my usually unflappable demeanor, let's not forget I worked for three other equally arresting men. Isaac may be the stoic, business-minded one, but the Gallos? Each of them brought their own brand of allure into the mix, making my work environment feel like the set of some unrealistically cast TV drama.

I decided it was high time for something stronger than workplace banter. I poured myself a modest glass of bourbon, justifying the mid-work libation by the fact that dinner was plated, desserts were safely tucked away in the fridge, and I was, for all intents and purposes, off the clock.

I took my glass and stepped onto one of the heated patios. The landscape stretched out before me, a tapestry of natural beauty that seemed almost surreal in its quiet majesty. This place was a sanctuary, a luxurious escape from the chaotic grind of city life. For a moment, as I sipped the smokey liquid, I allowed myself to simply exist in this pocket of serenity, letting the warmth from the bourbon settle my frazzled nerves.

But even bourbon couldn't fully drown out the nagging thoughts that had lodged themselves in the forefront of my mind. This job was too important, too good to mess up. Getting romantically tangled with one of my bosses—or God forbid, all four—was a one-way ticket to a very uncomfortable HR meeting, and likely unemployment.

"So what, Becca? You gonna trade in your dream job just because your bosses look like they've walked off the pages of GQ?" I asked myself, letting the biting chill of the air punctuate the point. "Yeah, that'll look great on a resume: Reason for leaving last job? Got caught up in a penthouse fantasy."

It was a dirty but undeniably intriguing thought, the kind better suited to private musings and absolutely not for workplace conduct. But that's all it could be—a thought, a fleeting temptation to be locked away in the fantasy vault of my mind, never to see the light of day.

I finished my bourbon, relishing the last drops as they rolled over my tongue and burned a comforting path down my throat. Then I glanced at my phone. Five minutes had passed since I told Isaac to have everyone in the dining room.

I took a deep breath, filling my lungs with the crisp

mountain air, and steadied myself. With my empty glass in hand, I walked back inside, ready to serve dinner, ready to put on the performance of composed, professional Becca.

But as I set my glass on the counter, I couldn't shake the image of Isaac's smile, the feel of his hand enveloping mine, and the almost-kiss that still tingled on my not-yet-touched lips. And so, as I entered the dining room, my steps confident and my face the picture of composure, I carried with me a pocketful of 'what-ifs,' carefully tucked away but burning hotter than ever.

CHAPTER 8

ARCHER

I watched her from the head of the table, her eyes still holding that glint of mischief that had sparked in our earlier conversation. She had a natural charisma about her, a blend of warmth and wit that drew people in, myself included. And I didn't like being drawn in.

"Becca, please, join us for dinner," I said, my voice carrying the non-negotiable weight of a command rather than a request.

She looked up, her eyes meeting mine, clearly weighing the balance between professionalism and the casual intimacy of a shared meal. "I usually eat later," she began, but Vinnie and Luke were already chiming in.

"Nonsense. You should join us," Vinnie grinned.

"Absolutely," Luke added, his casual endorsement settling the matter.

Isaac finalized it with a soft but firm tone. "Breakfast and lunch are your call, but dinner should be a group affair. Please, join us each evening."

She laughed, her eyes dancing with a light that seemed to make the room a little brighter. "Well, when you put it like that, how could I refuse? Dining with you four is certainly a step up from eating alone in the kitchen."

As she detailed the evening's menu, her passion for food was evident. "We have roasted chicken, seasoned with rosemary and thyme. It's accompanied by garlic mashed potatoes and sautéed vegetables with almonds. And for dessert, we'll have apple crisp topped with vanilla ice cream."

I reached for the wine bottle and poured her a glass, my eyes never leaving hers. The liquid splashed like a momentary whirlpool of choices and consequences. For both of us.

"This is a particularly fine vintage," I began, my eyes still locked on hers. "It's a blend, mostly Cabernet Sauvignon, with a bit of Merlot and a touch of Cabernet Franc. You'll find it's well-balanced yet complex. The nose is rich, filled with notes of blackcurrant, cedar, and a subtle hint of anise. On the palate, it's bold but not overbearing, with layers of fruit, earth, and spice, all culminating in a long, elegant finish."

She looked at me, then at the wine, then back at me again. Her eyes widened for a moment before she broke into a grin. "You know, it's always a trip to see a man who looks like he could bench press a Buick talk about wine with the finesse of a sommelier."

I chuckled, the sound deeper than I'd intended. "Appearances can be deceiving. Just because someone excels in one world doesn't mean they can't appreciate the finer things in another. We all have our layers."

Her smile deepened, and she nodded as if acknowledging a point well made.

"Thank you, Archer," she smiled, taking the glass from my hand. Our fingers brushed for a second, but in that second, a current passed, a tension that felt like the drawing of a bowstring.

I nodded, careful to keep my expression unreadable. I liked to think of myself as a man in control, but there were things even I didn't have control over, things I couldn't push away, no matter how hard I tried. And damn it, she was rapidly becoming one of those things.

As I took my seat, I looked around at my brothers and Isaac, then at Becca. She was different, a welcome contrast to the power dynamics and boardroom tension that filled our days. She had a knack for cutting through the noise, for making things simple when they were anything but.

But the more I watched her — the way she laughed with Vinnie, the way she listened to Luke, and the way she teased Isaac — the more I realized things were about to get very complicated. And for the first time in a long while, I wondered if complicated could actually be a good thing.

Dinner unfolded like a scene out of a movie—a rarity for men like us who usually dined in silence or over the clatter of keyboards. The laughter flowed more freely than I'd heard in a long time. It was as if Becca had some kind of magical effect on us, even on Isaac, who usually kept his cards close to his chest.

When the topic turned to childhood stories, each of us chipped in. Vinnie recounted tales of misadventures with firecrackers, and Luke talked about the summer he tried to build a treehouse and ended up breaking his arm. Isaac surprised us all by reminiscing about family vacations by the lake, his face softening into a rare smile as he spoke. His parents had passed away, but it was clear the memories he'd formed with them were happy ones—pure, untarnished by time.

Becca put down her fork and looked around the table as if gauging how much to share before she spoke. "Okay, well, I guess it's my turn. My story takes place one Christmas when I was about ten. My brother, Mikey, was seven. My dad had passed away a few years prior, so it was just me, my mom, and Mikey."

She paused for a moment, her eyes glossing over as if she were seeing the scene replay in her mind. "Money was always tight, you know? My mom worked two jobs just to keep the lights on and food on the table. So, when Christmas rolled around, we knew better than to expect much."

Her eyes twinkled as she got to the heart of the story. "That year, Mom sat us down and told us we were only getting one gift for the family. Mikey and I didn't mind; we were just excited for Christmas. A few days later, Mom comes home with this furball of energy—a black lab puppy, tail wagging so fast it could probably power a small generator."

The group chuckled, and Becca's face broke into a wide smile. "We named her Sadie, and let me tell you, she was the queen of the house from that day on. Mom spent whatever she could spare on Sadie—food, toys, you name it. That Christmas, we didn't have any gifts under the tree other than Sadie, but we didn't care. That dog was spoiled rotten and we adored her."

She finished her story, her eyes meeting each of ours as if challenging us to judge her humble past. "That year taught me that sometimes the best gifts aren't the ones you unwrap. They're the ones that come bounding into your life, knocking over the Christmas tree and scattering ornaments everywhere, but filling your home with so much love you can't imagine life without them."

For a moment, the table was quiet. Then Isaac raised his glass. "To the best gifts," he said.

The glasses clinked, sealing a moment of shared understanding and deepened connection among us. And for the first time in a long time, I felt like I was part of something that extended beyond boardrooms and bottom lines. I looked at Becca, our eyes meeting for a brief second, and realized she was the best kind of chaos, the kind you didn't know you needed until it was right there, staring you in the face.

"So Becca, you must be a dog person then, huh?" Vinnie inquired, steering the conversation in a way only he could.

Becca grinned, "Oh absolutely. Cats are fine, but there's something about a dog's loyalty and goofiness that always wins me over."

Vinnie nodded and fired off another question, something about what she liked to do in her free time. She was into hiking, loved photography, and was a sucker for old movies. I found myself taking mental notes, storing away each detail like a treasure.

She fit into our group in a way no one had before. Yet, she was not just one of the guys—she was different, she was...more.

Dinner ended, the air still tinged with the honesty and laughter that filled the conversation. I could tell we all felt a connection to Becca—each of us having lost a parent in some way or another. There was something in the way she looked away when we toasted, something hidden behind those clear eyes.

I wished Vinnie would launch one of his humorous rants or Luke would go into his empathic investigator mode. But they didn't, and I sure as hell was not the one to dig. I'd always believed in letting people keep their secrets until they're ready to share.

When it was time to clean up, we all stood, nearly in unison, offering to help. She waved us off, her eyes flashing a determined look that said she was in her element.

" Let me do my job. The kitchen is my domain."

We all took our seats again, but I caught Isaac, Luke, and Vinnie sneaking glances at her as she moved gracefully around the dining room. I'd be lying if I said I wasn't doing the same. She owned the space, commanded it like a general leading troops into battle.

We freshened up our drinks and headed into the living room, the fire crackling as we sipped and thought. Conversation was light – no doubt we all had the same thing on our minds that we were trying to puzzle out.

"Alright, gents," she called out after what seemed like an eternity but was actually only about half an hour. "I'm going to shower and hit the sack. Early day tomorrow."

We all rose and said our good nights, each word heavy with something none of us voiced but we all felt—a unique blend of respect, intrigue, and something else I couldn't quite place. It was damn unnerving.

My footsteps were heavy as I walked down the hallway toward my bedroom, but my mind was even heavier. It was filled with thoughts of contracts, security details, and now, inexplicably, Becca. As I passed by her bedroom door, a soft sound caught my ear. A moan. Instinctively, I halted, every protective fiber in me going taut.

Was she sick? Hurt?

Then I heard her murmuring, soft and indecipherable at first, but gradually becoming clearer. She was saying our names—Isaac, Luke, Vinnie, and even mine. My brows furrowed, and then it hit me like a goddamn freight train what was actually happening behind the door.

Fuck.

My whole body tightened at the realization, blood

surging south in a primal, uncontrollable reaction. I clenched my fists to anchor myself. This was Becca, my employee, and any other line of thinking was absolutely forbidden.

Should I have gone in? Hell no. That was a line that, once crossed, offered no return. I might be an asshole, but I wasn't a monster. Should I tell my brothers? That was a more complicated question. On one hand, it was an invasion of her privacy; on the other, it confirmed what I'd suspected—there was an undercurrent, a tension felt not just by me but apparently by her as well.

I took a deep breath and forced myself to move, my boots feeling as though they were made of lead. I wasn't the sort of man who eavesdropped on a woman's most private moments, even if those moments involved fantasies about me.

I would talk to the guys. We had an unspoken agreement: we didn't mix business with personal matters. But then again, none of us had accounted for Becca to walk into our lives and cloud our judgment.

For the moment, I headed to my room, but I knew sleep would be elusive. My thoughts were a tangled mess of business, family, and now a woman who had unknowingly turned all of our worlds slightly but irrevocably askew. She wanted us. And whether we'd admit it or not, we wanted to know more about this woman who was as complex as she was captivating. But at what cost?

CHAPTER 9

VINNIE

Swirling the liquid in my glass, the scent of aged scotch hit my nose. It was a fragrance I equated with unwinding, and it was doing wonders for my mood.

The living room's ambient glow, courtesy of the fireplace, gave everything a soft touch. Luke and I were sprawled on the plush leather couches, our heads close, going over the week's agenda. Skiing, choice hiking spots, and some much-needed downtime for fishing. This was the kind of vacation I'd been yearning for. A break from the grind.

But my thoughts were interrupted when Archer, the brother I often dubbed "the thinker," walked in. It didn't escape my notice that something was off with him. There was a ripple in his usually calm demeanor, an anomaly I couldn't ignore.

"I thought you were headed to bed?"

"Couldn't sleep," he said with an odd look.

Sitting back, I shot him a curious look. "What's got you looking like the cat that swallowed the canary, bro?"

Archer's gaze darted around, eventually landing on the office door. "Where's Isaac?"

Luke rolled his eyes, sipping his scotch. "In the office. Buried in his work, as always."

Sighing, Archer took a seat opposite me, his features taut. "You guys won't believe what I stumbled upon."

I leaned in, my curiosity piqued. Archer wasn't one to get easily flustered, and I was certain this would be worth hearing.

Archer shot another glance toward the office, then, lowering his voice, he said, "I heard Becca... in her room. She was... enjoying herself. And saying our names."

For a split second, silence reigned. His words created an electric charge, an unspoken tension wrapping around us. The soft crackle from the fireplace was the only thing breaking the stillness.

Suppressing a chuckle, I smirked. "You're screwing with us, right?"

But the seriousness in Archer's eyes told me all I needed to know. "I'm not kidding."

Luke, carefully placing his glass on the table, asked, "All our names?"

Archer nodded slowly. "Every single one."

A rush of mixed emotions hit me. There was surprise, a flicker of excitement, and, if I dug deep, a dash of smug satisfaction. "It's a fine line," I mused aloud. "On one hand, she's our employee. But on the other..."

Luke jumped in, "She's obviously attracted to us too."

Rubbing the back of my neck, I took a moment to gather my thoughts. "Whatever Becca does in her private moments is her business. But knowing this? It adds a new variable to the equation."

Archer looked tormented. "I should've minded my own business. But what do we do now?"

After a thoughtful pause, I answered, "We keep this to ourselves. It's her place to come to us if she ever wants to. Until then, it's business as usual."

Luke gave a nod of agreement. "It won't be easy, but her privacy is paramount."

Finishing my scotch, its warmth provided little comfort against the newfound turmoil. "This vacation's going to be more intriguing than any of us anticipated."

As the weight of our shared secret loomed over us, the stillness of the room was broken by the distinct sound of the office door clicking open. Isaac stepped in and his knack for reading a room had his brows puckered together. His sharp eyes darted between us, immediately picking up on the shift in the atmosphere.

"You three seem awfully intense for just vacation planning," he commented dryly, his eyes finally settling on me. Damn, he was good.

Luke shifted in his seat, glancing at Archer, as if silently begging him to take the lead. Archer cleared his throat, looking unusually uncomfortable. "It's... a bit of a situation," he started hesitantly, recounting his recent discovery about Becca.

He told Isaac about what he'd heard and how she'd mentioned each one of our names. There was no doubt what she'd been fantasizing about.

Isaac listened, his face betraying no emotion. His brow slightly furrowed, and when Archer finished, he took a deliberate breath. "No. Absolutely not," he stated crisply. "She's an employee. Getting involved with her could land us in a lawsuit nightmare. Not to mention what it'd do to our reputation."

His practicality was both a blessing and a curse, but I couldn't hold my tongue any longer. "Isaac, come on," I scoffed, leaning back into my seat, trying to keep my voice smooth and level, but there was an edge to it, unmistakable even to my ears. "We're not animals. It's not like we're going to corner her. Not a single one of us would ever force her into anything."

Luke chimed in, his tone firm. "If she says no, then it's a no. Full stop."

Isaac pinched the bridge of his nose. "It's not that simple. Perception is everything. If even a whisper of it got out, the ramifications could be damaging, especially in this climate."

"I get where you're coming from," I said, choosing my words with care. "But isn't this also about mutual respect? Becca isn't just some naive intern. She's sharp, intuitive, and knows how to handle herself. If she ever felt uncomfortable, she'd let us know and we'd address it."

Archer, ever the peacemaker, tried to broker a middle ground. "Look, we're not jumping into anything. We're just processing what I heard. I agree with Isaac, we need to be careful. But Vinnie's got a point too."

Isaac glared at me, as if he could transfer the weight of his responsibility onto my shoulders through sheer will. "This isn't some fling, Vinnie. This could have consequences."

I smirked, the irony not lost on me. "Isn't that the point of a vacation? To escape consequences for a while?"

He shot me a look that could freeze molten lava. "You know what I mean."

Sighing, I stood up, stretching. "Look, we all know where we stand. It's a delicate situation, but we're not rookies. We'll handle it with maturity."

I leaned back, staring at the amber liquid in my glass and let the weight of the silence rest for a moment before responding, "Isaac, from what I've seen, I don't think she'd be uncomfortable with us at all."

Archer nodded in agreement, casting a sidelong glance at our friend.

Isaac, not one to be easily swayed, ran a hand through his hair, frustration evident on his face. " She makes it awfully hard to resist." There was a flicker of something in his eyes, a hint of vulnerability. "But resist we must."

I chuckled, more out of disbelief than humor. "Really? You think we should just deny what's so palpably there? Let's give her the choice, at least."

Archer's voice rose, emphasizing his agreement, "Exactly. Who are we to decide for her?"

Isaac's jaw clenched, a physical display of his resolve. "It's about the company, Vin. Always has been. We've worked too damn hard to let anything threaten it."

With a smirk, I shot back, "Come on, Isaac. It's not just about the company, is it? I've seen the way you look at her. The way all of us look at her. And it's not with boardroom eyes. It's deeper than that."

His eyes flashed, but his voice was controlled. "The company has provided for us all these years. We can't throw that away on a whim. She's an employee. We have responsibilities."

Archer, the balance between Isaac's caution and my brazenness, stepped in. "Isaac, the company isn't everything. We're more than just the titles on our office doors."

Isaac shook his head, the lines of worry on his forehead more pronounced than ever. "But to risk everything for what? A few days of fun?"

I stood up, my voice smooth yet filled with conviction,

"It's not just a few days of fun and you know it. There's a connection. An energy. Why deny something that feels so right?"

Isaac took a deep breath, his hands resting on his hips. "It's not as simple as that. And it's not just about me. What if things don't work out? What then?"

Archer sighed, running a hand over his face. "We're adults. We deal with it. Like we always have. Like we always will."

The air was thick with tension, unspoken emotions, and the weight of decisions to be made. It wasn't just about Becca. It was about the balance of power, trust, and priorities. Three brothers, bound by blood and business, now navigating uncharted territory with their best friend.

Luke cleared his throat, drawing our attention to him. When he stood up, the room seemed to hush in response, waiting. Over the years, I had grown accustomed to valuing his perspective, knowing that he always seemed to find the path that straddled caution and opportunity.

His voice was calm, even-handed. "I think you're all right in your own ways. Isaac, your concerns about the company are valid. It's our livelihood. It's our family legacy. It's more than just numbers on paper—it's our blood, sweat, and tears."

I watched as Isaac nodded, appreciative of Luke's acknowledgment.

Luke continued, "However, Vinnie, Archer, you're also correct. Becca isn't some naive girl. She's a grown woman. From what we've all seen and felt, I believe she's capable of understanding the nuances of whatever situation might arise."

I grinned, finding solace in Luke's words. But it was what he said next that captured my complete attention.

"But here's my suggestion," Luke continued, his gaze fixed on each of ours in turn. "Let's let her make the first move. If she does nothing, we do nothing. We respect her choice, her agency. Let the ball be in her court."

Archer immediately voiced his agreement, "Sounds fair to me. Let her lead."

I raised my glass, nodding. "I'm in. Let's see where this goes, but on her terms."

Isaac, ever the contemplative one, looked pensive, his brow furrowed. "I still have my reservations, but if this is the course we're taking, I can get behind it. With one condition."

We all looked at him expectantly.

"We don't act on anything unless we're all in agreement. Every step of the way," he emphasized.

It was a fair point. Involving ourselves with Becca wasn't just an individual venture. It would affect all of us and our relationships with each other. Ensuring that every step was taken with a unanimous vote, so to speak, was a smart way to navigate these treacherous waters.

"Agreed," I said.

Luke nodded, "Fair enough."

Archer raised his glass, "To understanding and respect."

Isaac's gaze lingered on each of us for a moment longer, probably trying to ascertain our sincerity. Finally, he relented, raising his glass as well.

We toasted, the weight of the decisions and the future paths that lay before us clear in our minds. The evening had started as a simple chat among brothers and friends, but it had evolved into so much more. Whatever was to come, we were in it together.

CHAPTER 10

LUKE

The day dawned with a palpable tension in the air, so thick you could slice it with a knife. Every step, every word seemed laden with an intensity that had evolved overnight. As the self-appointed mediator among the four of us, I observed, weighing the exchanges with careful precision.

Vinnie, smooth as always, seemed to find innumerable reasons to be near Becca—his fingers brushing her arm as they discussed the day's itinerary, or the fleeting touch to the small of her back as he escorted her to a room, or even the gentle grip of her hand as he handed her something trivial. It was subtle but obvious... to a discerning eye.

Archer's actions mirrored Vinnie's, yet he brought his own brand of charm to the table. The playful nudges, the exaggerated leans to whisper something inconsequential in her ear, the lingering glances. It was a dance of attraction and subtle invitations.

I couldn't deny the effect it was having on Becca. Her skin flushed a delicate shade of rose each time one of them made contact. The way her eyes shone a tad brighter, her lips curved in a near-permanent smile. She responded to their gestures, a gentle touch here, a soft laugh there.

Yet as the dance continued in the living areas of our expansive home, Isaac had made himself scarce. I noticed he'd chosen the sanctuary of his office over the bustling interactions of the day. At first, I considered it a mere coincidence, but when he took his meals in the solitude of his workspace, the pattern became obvious. Perhaps he was attempting to distance himself, trying to minimize any potential complications.

During one of these mealtimes, Becca entered Isaac's den, and my curiosity was piqued. Their conversation was a murmur, the words unintelligible from where I stood, but the emotions weren't. Becca's laughter rang clear, a lilting tune that seemed to echo with joy and, dare I say, flirtation. It wasn't long before Isaac's own deep chuckle joined the mix.

I leaned against a nearby wall, considering the implications. Isaac, the most guarded among us when it came to Becca, seemed to have dropped his walls, even if momentarily. Was it the confines of the office, a safe space for him, that made him more susceptible? Or was it the genuine connection they might be forging?

The rest of the day progressed in a similar vein—charged interactions, lingering touches, stolen glances.

As the sun dipped below the horizon, casting the house in a warm, golden hue, I took a moment to reflect. Our pact to let Becca lead was holding strong. Yet the unfolding events of the day made one thing abundantly clear—while we might wait for her to make the first overt move, none of us, not even Isaac, could deny the pull she had on us.

The heart of the home, the dining area, was alight with the sounds of laughter and clinking glasses as the evening sun painted the room in shades of amber. As we settled around the dining table, the aroma wafting from the kitchen made it evident that Becca had prepared something special for dinner.

She walked in holding a large serving dish, a proud smile gracing her lips. "Gentlemen," she began, her voice dripping with anticipation, "I hope you're as hungry as I am. Tonight, I've prepared a slow-cooked beef bourguignon. It's tender beef chunks marinated in red wine and slowly simmered with carrots, onions, and mushrooms. The sauce is thick, infused with fresh herbs and a hint of bacon." She set the dish down with a flourish, the steam rising in delicate tendrils.

We dug into our meal and the conversation flowed, some of it laced with barely contained innuendos.

Becca took it all in stride. Her laughter rang out, genuine and unforced. But there was a subtle change in her demeanor, a heightened awareness not present before. Her cheeks, usually a soft pink, now held a deeper flush. Every movement, from the way she leaned in to listen to a comment to the deliberate manner in which she sipped her wine oozed sensuality. Her eyes, those expressive windows, flitted from one man to the next, holding each gaze a second longer than necessary, communicating unspoken promises and shared secrets.

At one point, as she reached across the table to pass a dish, her fingers brushed against mine. The contact was brief, almost incidental, but the electric charge it sent through me was undeniable. And it didn't help matters that she'd chosen a top low enough that each lean forward gave me a stunning view of her flawless cleavage. She caught me looking once, but the devilish smirk she made in response sent the message that she was more than happy to let me stare.

The night progressed in a mix of hearty food, playful banter, and simmering tension. Becca's secretive smile hinted at hidden depths and unexplored desires; it seemed permanently etched on her face.

As dessert was served and the last of the wine was poured, I reflected on the turn our vacation had taken. What was meant to be a relaxing getaway had morphed into a heady exploration of boundaries and desires. At the epicenter of it all was Becca, a force of nature who had, in no uncertain terms, shaken up our carefully orchestrated lives.

As the main course started to wind down, Becca, with a glint of mischief in her eyes, addressed the table. "Now, I have to confess, while I might know my way around the kitchen, when it comes to wine, Archer insisted on taking the reins for tonight." She cast a wry, teasing glance at him. "Apparently, my choice of red was a 'novice selection'?" She used her fingers to make air quotes.

A mix of chuckles echoed around the table. Archer, with a smirk and a raised eyebrow, took up the challenge immediately. He swirled the dark liquid in his glass, letting the deep ruby hue catch the light. Holding it up to his nose, he took a deep breath, as if trying to unravel the wine's secrets.

"Well," he began, with an air of faux solemnity, "when pairing with a dish as rich and robust as beef bourguignon, one simply must opt for a wine that can hold its own. This," he gestured grandiosely to the bottle, "is a 2015 Château Mouton Rothschild. A Bordeaux blend, predominantly Cabernet Sauvignon, that hails from Pauillac in France."

He took a contemplative sip, letting it sit on his palate before continuing. "It boasts a bold, full-bodied profile. On the nose, you'll find notes of black currants, violets, and a touch of cedar. As for the palate," he paused for dramatic effect, "layers of blackberries and cherries, underpinned by nuances of mocha and graphite. The finish is long and velvety with a hint of spiced oak."

The table was silent for a moment, everyone processing Archer's verbose description. Then Vinnie chimed in, "So... it's a good wine, yeah?"

Becca let out a hearty laugh. "That's one way to put it."

After the main course, Becca served a decadent molten lava cake, the rich chocolate oozing out with every spoonful, complemented by a dollop of vanilla bean ice cream on the side. Every bite was an exquisite dance of warm, gooey chocolate with cold, creamy vanilla. Clearly, Becca had outdone herself again, and everyone around the table was in a state of sweet euphoria.

The chatter of cutlery and glasses faded as everyone indulged in their dessert, murmurs of appreciation filling the air. Once the last spoonfuls were savored, the group began gathering their plates and glasses, moving in unison toward the kitchen. This time, she didn't protest our offer of help.

As Becca rinsed off a dish, she looked over her shoulder with a playful smile. "I was thinking of taking a dip in the hot tub. Anyone care to join me?" she inquired, her voice carrying a tone that hinted at more than just a casual soak.

Archer and I exchanged glances, a silent conversation transpiring between us. We could sense the undertone in her invitation. The hot tub was a space of intimacy, a location oozing sensuality. It could very well be Becca's way of gauging reactions, of testing waters yet to be traversed.

Isaac, his face unreadable but his voice pointed, responded, "No thanks." He held her gaze for a moment, a silent message passing between them before he handed her the pot from the side dish.

Vinnie grinned cheekily. "Sounds like fun," he said, clearly already visualizing the scene.

With a smirk and a sparkle in his eye, Archer added, "I'll bring out a bottle of wine. We can keep the party going."

I remained silent, mulling over the situation, calculating the potential outcomes, risks, and benefits. It was my nature to consider every angle before jumping in.

"I'll need about twenty minutes to clean up here," Becca informed us, a hint of anticipation in her voice. "Then I'll head upstairs to change."

Vinnie, ever the eager beaver, immediately headed out to the deck to get the hot tub going. I began my search through the cabinets, finally finding a set of plastic glasses suitable for outdoor use.

The door to the office slammed shut with an echoing thud, a clear indicator of Isaac's internal tempest. My footsteps were quieter, deliberate, as I trailed after him. He was my best friend, and whatever chasm had formed between his desires and his actions needed addressing. As I pushed the door open, I found him, his back rigid, hands gripping the edge of his desk.

"Why are you so against this, Isaac?" I began, voice level, measured. "If she's showing interest, why should we hold ourselves back?"

Isaac's sharp intake of breath was the only sound in the room for a moment. He looked up, and the raw emotion in his eyes momentarily took me aback. This wasn't just about Becca. It ran deeper.

"What's going on?" I pressed.

His voice trembled as he responded. "Becca... she makes me feel things. The way I felt when I first met Mindy. I can't—I won't—go down that path again."

The revelation was unexpected. I leaned back against the door, processing the weight of his confession. Mindy had been Isaac's first real love, and her betrayal had left scars that ran deep. Emotionally, he'd been on lockdown ever since, and I hadn't realized just how deep those feelings still went.

"I've never been in love, Isaac," I admitted, "so I can't claim to understand exactly what you're going through. But you can't keep running from these feelings. It's tearing you apart."

He exhaled deeply, pinching the bridge of his nose. "It's not just about the potential for love, Luke. It's the potential for pain."

I approached him slowly, placing a reassuring hand on his shoulder. "I get it. But you can't live in the shadow of what-ifs. If you're not comfortable with this, then step back. No one's forcing you into anything."

His eyes met mine, searching for understanding. "And what if she doesn't want this, any of it? What then?"

"If Becca isn't on board, it stops. Period," I affirmed. "But I have a feeling she's intrigued. And if there's mutual consent, we're adults capable of making our own decisions. We'll respect her boundaries, and each other's."

Isaac looked lost in thought, weighing the emotional risks against the potential for something meaningful. The weight of the past versus the allure of the present.

"We'll be in the hot tub," I added softly. "Join us if you

want. But don't do it for us, or even for her. Do it for your-self. Whatever you decide, it's okay."

With that, I left him alone with his thoughts, closing the door softly behind me. I hoped, for Isaac's sake, he'd find the strength to confront his past and embrace the possibility of a brighter, shared future.

CHAPTER 11

BECCA

The excitement zinged through my veins as I stepped into my room to change. The two-piece tankini I'd picked out for tonight was laid out on the bed. It was a choice piece; every time I wore it, I felt this unspoken power, a certain allure. It highlighted my curves perfectly, making me feel seductive and in control.

"Who needs Isaac anyway?" I whispered to myself, a touch of disappointment tinging my words.

Though I had secretly hoped he would be there, three out of four wasn't bad. And my, what a trio they promised to be.

A blush crept up my cheeks, memories of last night's wild fantasy playing in my mind. I'd never been one to daydream, but there was something about this setting, these men, that drew it out of me.

After ensuring everything looked just right, I threw on a hoodie to stave off the evening's chill, my legs bare. A quick glance in the mirror, a deep breath, and I was off.

It's just a hot tub hangout, I told myself. *No pressure. Nothing happens that you don't want to happen.*

But when I stepped out the back door, the sight before me was straight out of one of those romance novels I'd never admit to reading. Three striking men, each radiating a unique charm, awaited me. The soft patio lights only intensified their allure—Luke with his chiseled features, Vinnie with that ever-present mischievous grin, and Archer, whose intense gaze promised mysteries I was eager to uncover.

"You're late," Luke's voice slid over me, smooth and teasing.

I raised an eyebrow, smirking at his sarcasm. "Fashionably late is always in style."

Vinnie's laughter was infectious. "Always worth the wait," he commented, his eyes warm and inviting.

Archer held out a glass of wine. "For the belle of the ball," his voice, dripping with charm, whispered.

Our fingers brushed as I took the glass, and sparks flew, undeniable and intense.

Hiding behind a sip of the rich wine, I gathered my courage. "Where's Isaac?" I tried to sound casual, hoping my disappointment wasn't too evident.

A shared glance between Vinnie and Archer spoke volumes. "Work to catch up on," Vinnie finally replied. "But he wanted us to make sure you have a good time."

I grinned, the combined weight of their gazes thrilling me. "With you three? I doubt that'll be a problem." I pulled the hoodie off. As soon as I did, I could feel the heat of their stares as they gazed at the sight of my skimpy suit.

I felt so powerful.

Slipping into the hot tub, the warm water enveloping me, I felt the boundaries of our professional relationships start to blur. The stars overhead, the soft bubbles, their lingering looks—all of it promised an evening I wouldn't forget.

The warmth from the wine, amplified by the heated water, was dizzying.

With a playful smirk, Archer gently swirled the wine in his glass, allowing the deep ruby liquid to dance against the translucent edges.

"This, Becca, is a rather sensual wine," he began, his voice dripping with mischief, matching the wine's allure. "It's a 2015 Pinot Noir from a vineyard notorious for producing wines that... well, let's just say they're known to stimulate the senses."

I smiled. The sight of a big bruiser like Archer eloquently explaining the finer points of wine always made me grin.

He leaned a bit closer, and I could feel the heat emanating from his body, contrasting with the cool breeze of the night. "Notice its legs," he motioned toward the wine, letting it glide down the side of the glass. "Long, slender, and incredibly seductive." His gaze met mine with a wink.

I took a sip, and its warmth spread across my tongue.

"The first thing you'll probably notice," he continued, "is the soft, velvety texture. It's supple, wrapping around your palate much like a lover's embrace." He raised an eyebrow teasingly, making my cheeks flush.

"But it's not just about the initial touch," he whispered, leaning even closer. "It's about the layers. Dark cherries, blackberries, a hint of vanilla – it's complex, but every layer is perfectly balanced. A dance of flavors, each step bringing you deeper and deeper into its embrace, making you yearn for more."

He took a sip then, eyes locked onto mine, letting the moment linger, letting the innuendos hang in the air between us. "And just like a passionate evening, it leaves a lasting impression, a finish that lingers long after the initial encounter."

Taking Vinnie's outstretched hand, I felt a shiver run up my spine, which wasn't from the chilly evening air. With his guidance, I settled further into the bubbling water, placing myself strategically between him and Luke. The sensation of being surrounded, the heat from the water and their bodies close by, was electrifying.

I reveled in the moment, allowing myself to fully appreciate the situation. Three pairs of eyes, each radiating its own brand of intensity, fixed on me. It was thrilling, nerve-wracking, and so very new.

A breath escaped me, my attempt at steadying the fluttering sensation in my chest. But Vinnie caught on. "You okay, Becca?" His eyes, deep and concerned, searched mine.

The mix of wine, bubbling water, and adrenaline broke down any walls of restraint I had. Before I even realized what was happening, the words tumbled out. "So, what's the deal with your love lives?"

So much for subtlety.

Silence. Then Archer, always one to face a challenge head-on, slid closer, his hands coming to rest gently on my knees. The warmth of his touch contrasted with the cool exterior of his demeanor. His eyes held a playful gleam. "What exactly do you want to know, Becca?"

My mind raced, trying to form a coherent response. But before I could string together any words, Luke's voice, husky and tempting, whispered directly into my ear. The sensation of his warm breath against my skin sent a flurry of shivers down my spine.

Archer grinned. "How about we answer your question with a question?"

"Sure."

A pause.

"Do you want us?"

I nodded, barely able to find the words. "Yes. Yes, I do. All of you." I couldn't believe the words as they came out of my mouth. But there they were, in the open.

Luke moved over, leaning in. The feeling of his lips on the side of my neck sent shivers through me. His breath, warm and inviting, trailed down my skin, making my heart race. I closed my eyes for a moment, letting the sensation wash over me.

Vinnie's gentle touch on my chin snapped my eyes open, and he turned me toward him. His eyes searched mine for a brief moment before he leaned in. The softness of his lips took me by surprise, and I found myself leaning into the kiss. There was an unexpected tenderness to it, making it all the more intense.

Across the hot tub, Archer's mischievous grin had become serious, his eyes piercing. The sensation of his hands sliding up my legs brought me back to the present. My breathing quickened as his fingers delicately spread my legs apart. The gentle movement, combined with the depth of his gaze, held a silent question, offering me a final chance to halt things. Yet every cell in my body screamed for more, a need so profound I couldn't possibly deny it.

The only sounds were our breathing and the gentle ripple of water. It felt as if the world had stopped, the universe now revolving around this singular moment in time.

"What are we doing?" I managed to whisper, suddenly overwhelmed by the gravity of the situation. Yet even as I asked, my body instinctively leaned into their touches, craving their closeness.

"It's what you want, isn't it?" Luke whispered, his lips

tracing the curve of my ear. His words were both a question and a statement, and I couldn't find my voice.

"I... yes. But..."

"But?" Vinnie questioned softly, his fingers gently stroking my cheek.

"I don't want things to get weird between us," I admitted. "This is all so sudden, so unexpected. And I really like you guys."

Archer's fingers paused on my thigh, his gaze never leaving mine. "Life is unexpected, Becca. Sometimes, you just have to dive in and embrace the unpredictability. All the same, if it's too much..."

That was my cue to end things, if I wanted to. The men desired me like mad, but they were gentlemanly enough to give me an ejection lever to pull if it was more than I could handle. But I wanted them, and there were no doubts in my mind about it.

I nodded slowly, feeling a strange sense of calm wash over me. "Okay," I whispered, letting the weight of my decision settle. "I want this."

Luke pulled me closer, his lips seeking mine. The gentle caress of Vinnie's fingers and the warmth of Archer's touch combined to send my senses into overdrive.

Time seemed to stretch, moments blending seamlessly into one another. Everything else faded away as I lost myself in the intoxicating dance of lips, hands, and whispered promises.

The sensations were overwhelming. The cool night air seemed almost biting against my skin, especially in contrast to the heated water of the hot tub. Steam rose gently, drifting into the night sky, wrapping around us like a soft veil. I could barely process the whirlwind of emotions coursing through me; each touch, each look exchanged with the men, heightened the sensations.

Luke's lips lingered on the side of my neck, fingers danced along my collarbone, leaving trails of tingling warmth. Vinnie was on my other side, his touch a grounding presence. He turned my chin gently, our eyes meeting in a silent promise. His lips met mine in a tender kiss, full of a passion I hadn't experienced in so long. His hand moved underneath my top, taking hold of my breast and teasing my nipple. I reached under the water and took hold of his hard length, sighing at the sensation.

Archer, with his mischievous glint, had positioned himself right across from me. I could feel his gaze, intense and searching, as his hands slid slowly up my legs. Every movement was deliberate, giving me ample time to process, to decide. But there was no hesitancy in me. The desire was mutual.

As I reclined, the sensation of hands, strong yet gentle, caressed my skin. Luke's fingers trailed along my collarbone, igniting a fire within me. Archer's hands, always surprisingly soft for such a rugged man, slipped down my back, making me arch slightly in response. Vinnie's playful touches were unmistakable, his fingertips gliding along my thighs, teasing and tantalizing.

Their touches combined, weaving an intricate dance of desire over my body. I felt cherished, wanted, and alive in a way I had never experienced before.

Every whisper, every chuckle shared among the men, made me more aware of the burgeoning tension. The water seemed to ebb and flow with our combined breaths, in sync with the rhythm of their desires.

When the time came for the men to discard the last barriers of fabric separating them from the water, my anticipation peaked. One by one, the sight of them revealing their bare forms was a feast for my eyes. Their well-defined physiques, each distinct yet equally alluring, glistened under the ambient lights, casting shadows that teased my imagination. Their manhoods were impressive, thick and long and hard, my pussy clenching at the sight of them.

The steam from the tub rose, creating a dream-like veil around us. It was both intimate and surreal, the night, the water, and the three of them, all focused intently on me. I could feel the weight of their gazes, each one heavy with desire.

Vinnie's fingers traced patterns on my skin, igniting flames everywhere he touched. The gentle lapping of the water and the soft glow from the tub's lights created a sanctuary around us.

He wrapped his arms around me, his cock pressing against my belly. I couldn't resist him any longer, reaching down and taking hold of his prick and guiding it toward me, placing his head at my entrance.

"You ready?" he asked.

"So ready."

"Wait. Do we need...?"

I shook my head. "No. I'm on the pill." A warmth spread through me at his thoughtfulness. The men wanted me desperately, I could tell. But all the same, they wanted me to be comfortable.

"Please," I said. "Don't make me wait."

With that, he pushed inside. I threw back my head and moaned, his manhood filling me, stretching me in the most delicious way. Soon he had bottomed out, his many inches gone between my legs. As Vinnie and I became one, the outside world faded away. The raw intensity of the moment heightened my awareness of every sensation, every touch.

The other men, while respectful, watched intently, their gazes adding another layer of intensity to the experience. Archer and Luke, clearly affected, wore expressions of heat and desire, as if they couldn't wait for their turn.

It felt like we were in our own world, a bubble where time had paused, and the only thing that mattered was the here and now. Their touches, their words, the shared glances, all culminated in a crescendo of emotions and sensations.

Vinnie pushed harder and harder into me under the water, and it wasn't long before we were both on the verge of release.

"There!" I shouted. "Just like..."

I couldn't finish. A powerful orgasm rushed through me, my legs wrapping around Vinnie's waist and pulling him closer as I came. He joined me, his muscular body tensing as he drained himself deep inside me.

When it was over, we remained, intertwined in the water, the night casting a serene blanket over us. I rested against Vinnie, his heartbeat steady against me, while Luke's fingers continued to trace idle patterns on my arm, and Archer, with that ever-present smirk, winked at me from across the tub.

In that moment, it was clear this was just the beginning of something profound.

CHAPTER 12

ARCHER

Becca's face, flushed from her time with Vinnie, was a picture of satisfaction, but there was a hunger in her eyes that said she wasn't done yet. From my vantage point, I could see every curve, every arch of her back, and it was tantalizing. But I had to wait. It was Luke's turn.

"Your move," Vinnie smirked at Luke, a gleam of pride in his eyes. Luke, always the calm and collected one, didn't rush. He locked eyes with Becca and asked, "How do you want it?"

She hesitated for a moment, caught in the weight of decision, but then that familiar bold spark appeared in her eyes. "Surprise me," she replied, her voice dripping with anticipation.

A corner of Luke's mouth lifted in a half-smile. "Alright then." In a fluid movement, he turned Becca around in the water, positioning her to face away from him.

The moonlight gave a silver sheen to Becca's skin, making her look ethereal. Luke placed his hands on her waist, pulling her close, aligning their bodies just right. She tilted her head back, resting it against his shoulder, eyes closed in pleasure.

From where I sat, I could see every emotion play out on their faces. The passion, the anticipation, the trust. Luke thrust, and it wasn't long before the only sounds were the sloshing of the water and their synchronized breathing. I could see the tension building in Becca's form; her grip on the tub's edge tightened, her knuckles white. Her perfect, full breasts swayed as Luke drove into her again and again.

The crescendo built steadily, and soon Becca's moans echoed off the trees surrounding us. The culmination was powerful, a crashing wave of release that seemed to resonate through the water and into all of us watching.

Luke's own climax followed closely, his head thrown back, eyes tightly shut, his hands gripping the softness of her hips. The force of it seemed to pull the energy from his body, leaving him drained but satisfied.

The aftermath was a picture of raw emotion and connection. Becca, breathless and radiant, leaned heavily into Luke. Luke, for his part, wrapped his arms around her, pulling her close, providing warmth and comfort.

In the sultry haze of the hot tub, with steam all around us, it was hard to differentiate reality from fantasy. Vinnie had ignited the spark, and Luke had kindled the flame; now, as it was my turn, I felt the desire to make the experience unforgettable for Becca.

Positioning myself on the edge of the hot tub, I felt the cold sting of the winter air on my back, juxtaposed with the warmth from the bubbling water lapping at my legs. I stretched out my hand to Becca, beckoning her toward me. Without hesitation, her wet hands met mine, her fingers intertwining with mine securely.

From my vantage point, I watched as she moved with

purpose and grace, like a feline. She positioned herself over me, and I could feel the heat radiating from her, a palpable energy between us. I took a moment to admire her silhouette against the ambient lighting from the cabin: the arch of her back, the droplets of water tracing rivulets down her curves, the expectant look in her eyes.

Her descent onto me was slow, measured, allowing us both to savor every inch, every sensation. The steam from the tub formed a halo around her, making her seem both untouchable and entirely mine in that singular moment. The world beyond our entwined bodies faded, every sound muffled, every distraction blurred.

Her movements on top of me were rhythmic, hypnotic. I watched, fascinated, as her hair, heavy with moisture, cascaded over her shoulders, occasionally brushing my chest. With every undulation, the weight of her pressing down, taking me deeper, I felt a growing intensity. We locked eyes, and in them, I saw a myriad of emotions - lust, trust, challenge. I cupped her bouncing breasts with my hands, teasing her perfect, pink nipples, feeling them go hard.

The moment of release approached rapidly, but the journey to it felt drawn out, a testament to our connection. When it crashed over us, it did so with a magnitude that made everything else inconsequential. The world shrunk, there was just us, the steam, the water, and our shared climax.

In the aftermath, with her nestled against my chest, I felt a possessive urge, a desire to stake a claim, to leave an indelible mark on her memory. "Next time," I whispered, my voice husky with emotion, "I'm going to make you finish with just my mouth."

She pulled back to look at me, her eyes gleaming with

mischief and promise. "Challenge accepted," she murmured, sealing our pact with a searing kiss.

When we were all done and spent, smiles on our faces, I reached back and grabbed the Pinot Noir.

"Now," I said, offering the drink. "Who'd like seconds?"

CHAPTER 13

BECCA

The languor following the intensity of what had just happened between us all was both surreal and grounding. My heart still raced in my chest, and while the adrenaline slowly dissipated, the memories of every touch, every whispered word, played vividly in my mind. The soft bubbling of the hot tub was a gentle background track, and the night sky above, peppered with stars, made the scene almost otherworldly.

Vinnie's warm, solid chest pressed against my back, his arm securely around my waist. I could feel his rhythmic breathing syncing with mine. It was a silent testament to the bond we were forming, not just physically but emotionally as well.

"You know," Vinnie murmured, the hint of a chuckle in his voice, "if you fall asleep now and slip under, I'd have to play hero." The humor was evident, but the underlying protectiveness in his voice made my heart flutter.

Before I could retort, strong arms encircled me from the front. Luke, his face mere inches from mine, had that look - a mix of pride and concern.

"How about I take you upstairs? You look like you need a proper bed."

I smirked, nudging him slightly. "I think I can manage, Luke. I'm not as fragile as I look." But despite my words, Luke hoisted me up, cradling me in his arms with an ease that showcased his strength.

The transition from the warm water to the frigid outside air was immediate, and I shivered. Almost instinctively, a towel appeared over my shoulders. Archer gave me a knowing look, his eyes gleaming with amusement. "Told you it'd be cold."

As Luke navigated through the house, the warmth and familiarity of the environment began to sink in. The soft glow of the lights, the distant sounds of Vinnie and Archer discussing something in low tones, everything felt right.

Without missing a beat, Luke walked into my bedroom and straight into the adjoining bathroom. The plush rug felt good against my feet as he set me down. The room was bathed in soft lighting, highlighting the marble countertops and the vast shower.

Luke leaned in, turning the faucet, the sound of water starting to fill the room. Steam began to rise, and I could feel the heat emanating from the droplets. Before I could say anything, Luke's hand gently cradled my face, pulling me into a soft, lingering kiss. It was different from before - tender, reassuring.

"Need any help in there?" His voice was a husky whisper, the hint of playfulness evident.

The scent of the steam from the shower clouded the bathroom with warmth, both a balm and an invitation. Luke's offer had caught me off guard. As much as my body still hummed from earlier, my rational mind questioned the wisdom in pushing the limits. But when he promised with his unyielding confidence, my reservations began to melt.

"Not sure if I have it in me," I said. "You guys really know how to spend a girl's energy."

As soon as I said the words, however, I knew I wasn't done for the night.

"There's more left in you than you think, Becca," he whispered, a gentle challenge.

"Hmm, maybe you're right. One way to find out, huh?"

I allowed him to guide me into the spacious shower, the marble cool beneath my feet but quickly warming up with the water's embrace. A bench, carved seamlessly from the same stone, beckoned invitingly. Luke gently ushered me to it, his eyes never leaving mine. His body was something else, looking just as carved from stone as the rest of the shower.

"Let's start with something nice and relaxing," he said.

As I settled onto the bench, Luke dropped gracefully to his knees in front of me. The significance of that act wasn't lost on me; this dominant man was putting himself in a vulnerable position for my pleasure. And when his mouth met the sensitive juncture of my thighs, I gasped, the world narrowing to the sensation of his tongue and the rhythm he set.

It didn't take long for him to draw that keen edge of pleasure from me, his name slipping from my lips in a breathless exclamation. The intimacy of the moment, the overwhelming sensation, left me trembling. I came hard against his mouth, my body shaking as I slipped my fingers into his hair.

"See?" he asked when I was done, his mouth glistening with my arousal. "You had a little more in you after all."

His hands, however, didn't stop their gentle ministrations. The tender care he took as he helped me wash my hair, massaging my scalp, the slow circles he made down my back, arms, and legs, washing away the fatigue and tension, was as intimate as any act we'd shared so far. My eyes drooped heavily, and I leaned into his touch, savoring every second.

Once we stepped out, a plush towel enveloped me, the softness against my skin a stark contrast to the wet slickness from before. Luke patted me dry with care, every touch underlining the depth of connection we'd shared.

In the soothing dimness of my bedroom, I rummaged through my dresser, pulling out a soft pair of pajamas. They whispered against my skin as I slipped into them, a comforting embrace.

With the night deepening outside, the silvery sheen of moonlight filtered through the curtains. Luke, now wrapped in a towel, approached the edge of the bed. Bending down, his lips met mine in a chaste kiss, a simple gesture that held a world of sentiment.

Before I could settle into the inviting embrace of sleep, the door to my room eased open. My heart rate quickened, but not in fear. In the doorway stood Vinnie and Archer, fully dressed, their expressions unreadable in the dim light.

The three of them together painted a picture of unity, brotherhood, and shared understanding. Luke, his hair damp and clad only in a towel, stood with them, a part of this mosaic of masculinity.

Silence settled in the room, the only sound our collected breaths. They didn't need words. Their mere presence was a testament to the connection we had built, the unspoken pact formed between us.

The residual intensity of the night continued to pulse

within me, each man leaned down to place a soft, lingering kiss on my forehead. Those kisses were a silent symphony of gratitude, echoing with the beauty of vulnerability shared and boundaries surpassed.

My body, already settling into the comfort of my bed, yearned for the closeness that had become so integral to the evening. I wanted them near, their steady heartbeats, the warmth of their skin — a reminder that the magic we'd woven together was real.

"I wish one — or all of you — would stay," I murmured, the words spilling out in a half-whisper, laced with a mixture of boldness and trepidation.

Archer chuckled softly, his lips curling in his signature smirk. "This is a California king, right? We should fit."

With a grace that belied their stature, Vinnie and Archer slipped into the bed on either side of me, the sheets rustling softly in protest. The contrasting warmth from both sides enveloped me, one radiating steady strength, the other a fiery passion.

Luke, meanwhile, hesitated, giving us a quizzical look before disappearing, presumably to change. When he returned, the playful camaraderie between the brothers was palpable. Vinnie teased him, his voice dripping with mischief. "Looks like you missed your spot right here," he tapped the mattress next to me, winking.

Luke rolled his eyes but couldn't hide the amused smile tugging at his lips. "Room on the other side?" he asked Archer, who simply scooted over with a shrug, making space. Luke's warmth soon joined the comforting cocoon the others provided.

In that dreamy haze of contentment, their steady breaths lulling me, my thoughts strangely drifted to the one face missing from this tableau. Isaac. His mysterious demeanor, the silent strength he exuded, the hints of depths unexplored — it all drew me in. Tonight would have been different with him, maybe even more profound. A pang of longing struck me, the wish that he too had been a part of this shared moment.

CHAPTER 14

ISAAC

Thirty minutes earlier...

From the seclusion of the dimly lit room, I leaned against the glass, allowing the cold touch to counteract the fire coursing through my veins. Becca, stunning Becca, was out there, laughing, smiling, her skin glistening from the water of the hot tub. Every curve of her body told a tale of allure, and as the other guys surrounded her, basking in her magnetic pull, desire twisted inside me like a blade.

I had been in situations of temptation before, had faced down challenges that would break lesser men, but the sight of Becca draped in moonlight was almost enough to undo all my stoic resolve. I envisioned taking her by the hand, feeling her fingers intertwine with mine, guiding her gaze toward me, and stealing those pleasured moans for myself.

But I had my reasons. Reasons that weighed heavy, forming a barrier I wasn't sure I could, or should, ever cross. As head of the company, as the one who always needed to be on guard, I couldn't afford the risk, not with her. She wasn't just another fling or a short-lived temptation; with

Becca, the stakes were high. There was a fragility to my heart I hadn't admitted to anyone, a fear of being vulnerable, of being seen as less than the dominant, in-control boss they all knew. A fear of being hurt by someone as pure and genuine as her.

So I found solace in the shadows, away from the sensual noises and tantalizing visions. The intricate dance of pleasure playing out before my eyes was torturous, making me question every decision, every step I had taken to keep my distance. A gnawing sensation tugged at me, whispering what I was missing, what I could be a part of if I just let go of my inhibitions.

But I retreated, my feet leading me back deeper into the office. The comfort of the familiar greeted me: dark mahogany, the intoxicating scent of old books, and the gleaming bar counter. As I poured myself a glass of aged scotch, the amber liquid shimmered, promising a temporary reprieve from the turmoil inside. The first sip was a balm, smooth and fiery, setting my insides alight and numbing the edges of my longing.

The office was my sanctuary, a place where I could shed the facades and just be Isaac — not the boss, not the alpha, just a man with his thoughts and a drink in his hand. As I settled into the plush leather chair, the weight of the evening pressed down on me. I considered the reports, the figures, anything to detract from the image of her. Yet her laughter echoed, a siren song I couldn't escape.

I knew sleep wouldn't come easy tonight. There was a battle raging within, between the man who wanted to claim, to taste, to touch, and the leader who knew the costs of indulgence. For now, duty won out.

As the minutes ticked by, the quiet hum of the computer was overshadowed by the sounds of muffled laughter and whispered conversations filtering in from the corridors. The soft creaking of floorboards, the rustle of fabric, the muted sound of footsteps—each was a vivid reminder of the scene that had unfolded outside, the scene I'd deliberately chosen to remove myself from. It was like salt on an open wound, one I hadn't even acknowledged until now.

I leaned back, sinking into the cushioned chair, attempting to immerse myself in the world of spreadsheets and pie charts. It was supposed to be therapeutic, an escape into the mundane world of numbers where human emotions could not reach. But the tendrils of memory, unbidden and powerful, began to wrap around my consciousness.

The sharp sting of betrayal flashed before my eyes, a wound that had never quite healed. Mindy. The name was enough to conjure up a whirlwind of emotion. Her laughter, the warmth of her touch, the whispered promises—how had it all gone so wrong? The bitterness of our last moments together still lingered, an aftertaste I could never quite wash away. The moment I'd found her with him, with *him* of all people, it had shattered a part of me. My supposed friend, the one person I had trusted outside the tight-knit circle of the Gallo brothers. The treachery of it was a blow that still sent ripples through me.

And the worst part? The blame she'd heaped upon me, as if my dedication to my work, my relentless drive, was a justification for her infidelity.

"You're never around, Isaac!" she had yelled, tears streaming down her face, her words a mixture of anger and guilt. "You love your work more than you ever loved me." Those words had stung, tearing open old insecurities, questioning my worth, my priorities.

My grip on the crystal tumbler tightened. I could feel the edges practically cutting into my palm, a slight pain, a small reminder that I was still here, still real, still capable of feeling. I took a deep sip, letting the scotch burn a path down my throat, grounding me in the present.

But every time I closed my eyes, the faces of the brothers and Becca danced before them, bringing forth a different kind of pain, one of longing, of missed opportunities. Here I was, battling the ghosts of my past, while a future — uncertain, alluring — beckoned from just outside my door. But for now, I was trapped in my memories, imprisoned by the scars of past betrayals.

I sipped the scotch, memories flooding my mind of that day...

In New York, at my old apartment in Hell's Kitchen, I'd walked in on them together. Now Clay, my former friend, was back, having arrived with Mindy to pick up the rest of her things. He'd smooth-talked his way into my apartment, telling me the sooner he got her things and was gone, the sooner it would all be over.

But once the reality hit that he was in my home, I could barely keep the rage at bay. My knuckles turned white, clenched so hard they threatened to break the skin, as Clay sauntered out of my bedroom with an infuriating nonchalance. His careless gaze scanned the room and settled on me with a mocking smirk. It took every ounce of self-control not to launch myself at him. Every inch of me screamed for retribution, for a chance to mete out the pain I felt deep inside.

"Hurry it up, asshole. I want you good and gone," I ground out through gritted teeth.

Clay shrugged, his casual demeanor making my blood

boil even more. "Patience, brother. Not good for your heart to get pissed off."

The audacity of the man. To walk into my sanctuary, the place I'd built with the woman he'd stolen, as if he had every right. It felt like a slap in the face, a raw, stinging reminder of the wound that had yet to heal.

I was prepared to let it go. But he pushed me too far.

"Trust me, man, I'm eager to get out of here too. Got a busy day with Mindy ahead... and night." He followed up his words with a smirk. And I was done.

Without another word, I lunged at him. Vinnie, who'd been there with me, intercepted me just in time, wrapping his arms around my chest in a vice-like grip.

"Enough, Isaac!" he bellowed, dragging me back. His voice, firm and commanding, was enough to pull me back from the precipice, but not enough to quell the storm of anger inside me.

She appeared, entering the front doors as she'd done so many times before.

Mindy's voice sliced through the tense atmosphere. "You really are an asshole, you know that, Isaac?" Her eyes, once soft and adoring, now shot daggers at me. She didn't even look like the woman I fell in love with. Her face was contorted with rage, her eyes aflame with indignation.

She rushed to Clay's side, shooting me a withering look. "You always said you loved me," she spat, her voice dripping with venom, "but all you know is *work* – work and jealousy. I pity the woman who falls for you next."

That stung more than any physical blow. With Clay's arm slung over her shoulder, they made their way to the door, leaving Vinnie and me in a room thick with tension and unresolved emotions.

Vinnie let go of me, his face a picture of sympathy and concern. "You okay, bro?"

I didn't answer. My thoughts were a whirlwind, a cacophony of pain, anger, and regret. Watching Mindy leave with Clay was the final nail in the coffin of our relationship. The love I'd thought was unbreakable had shattered into a million pieces. And as I stood there, in the echoing silence of my once-shared home, I swore to never let anyone get that close again.

As I leaned back in the familiar comfort of my leather office chair, memories of Mindy and Clay pressed heavily on my chest. The aftertaste of the scotch I sipped was a bitter reminder of countless nights I'd tried to numb my pain. Back then, the golden liquid was my escape, a temporary relief from the heartache.

There were nights, blurred and hazy, when I'd return home, eyes barely focusing, only to find one of the Gallo brothers waiting for me. They saw me at my lowest, bearing silent witness to my shattered soul. Archer, with his unspoken strength; Vinnie, the jester, always trying to make me smile; and Luke, grounding me with his wisdom.

I glanced at the scotch bottle on my desk. It was more than half-empty, but its pull had faded. The Gallo brothers had seen to that, making me realize such solace was fleeting.

And in the midst of my recovery, Becca had come into my life. Her very presence was like sunlight breaking through storm clouds. I found myself irresistibly drawn to her, yet every time I edged closer, the ghosts of my past held me back. The sting of Mindy's betrayal was still fresh, making the idea of opening up again a daunting prospect.

I swiveled my chair, gazing out at the night bathed in moonlight. The serenity outside was in stark contrast to the storm within me.

"I'm not her," a voice echoed in my mind. It was Becca, speaking words she'd never said to me but words I could imagine her saying. Even though I never spilled my fears, it seemed she sensed them.

A sigh escaped my lips. Was I ready to put my heart on the line again? Could I let Becca in?

One thing was undeniable: Becca was the antithesis of Mindy. Where Mindy had been cold and selfish, Becca was all warmth and generosity. Where Mindy sought to pull me down, Becca lifted me up.

I took a deep breath, grappling with the emotions surging within. The anguish, the trepidation, the budding hope. And as I exhaled, I made a vow: to let love in again, to take the risk, however formidable it might be. Because the prospect of true happiness with Becca was worth braving potential heartbreak.

I reached the hallway, the soft amber light from Becca's room illuminating the corridor. From the open door, I could see her, a picture of contentment nestled among the Gallo brothers. The soft, rhythmic sounds of their breathing, punctuated by the faint rustling of sheets, created an almost hypnotic lullaby.

Rather than being pulled into the gentle reverie, an unexpected pang gripped my chest. Jealousy. A bitter, foreign taste. I'd always considered myself above such emotions, especially given our unconventional situation. But seeing her there, so at ease, I felt an undeniable urge to be part of that tableau, to be right beside her.

As I hesitated at the threshold, I considered the idea of joining them. Would it be a welcome addition or an intrusion? The Gallo brothers had always been open-minded, our bond deeper than most families. But this...this was uncharted territory for all of us.

Would they welcome me into the fold, make space for me beside Becca? Or would they sense my hesitation, my internal conflict, and wish I'd stayed away?

Pushing off the door frame, I made my way to my bedroom. My thoughts raced, tangled and chaotic. I'd always been the logical one, the one who relied on reason over emotion. Yet here I was, gripped by an unfamiliar whirlwind of jealousy and longing.

My fingers drummed a restless beat on the wooden surface of my nightstand, echoing the turmoil inside. Should I talk to Becca? Lay bare my feelings and fears? Or should I just take the plunge, let go of my reservations and let myself be part of this?

I sank into my bed, the weight of my thoughts pushing me down. But even as I was consumed by this inner struggle, a singular realization rose above the noise: I needed to heal. Not for Becca, not for the Gallo brothers, but for myself. Until I could reconcile with my past, confront the demons of my betrayal, I couldn't hope to be part of any future, however tempting it might be.

Pulling the covers close, I tried to drown out the sounds coming from Becca's room. But they persisted, a gentle reminder of what could be, of what I was missing out on. Tomorrow, I decided, would be a new day. A day to confront, to heal, to move forward. I just hoped it wasn't too late.

CHAPTER 15

BECCA

The familiar chime of my phone pulled me from my dreams, the sensation of the previous night still lingering on my skin. With a lazy smile, I stretched out, feeling every delicious ache. The bed beside me was empty, the cool sheets a testament to the Gallo brothers' early departure.

I groped around, fingers finally closing around the phone. The screen displayed Mom and I answered with a still sleepy, "Hello?"

"Becca, honey! How are you? Did I wake you up?" Mom's voice rang out, the same energetic tone I'd known all my life.

"Kind of, but I needed to get up anyway," I said, pushing strands of hair from my face. "What's up?"

"I wanted to remind you about Christmas, dear. You're coming home, right? You promised!" There was a hint of desperation in her voice. Mom and I shared a bond unlike any other. She was both my parent and my confidante.

I laughed, pulling the covers up to my chin. "For the

hundredth time, yes. I'll be there on Christmas Eve. My flight lands at one pm. Why do you keep asking?"

She gave a secretive chuckle. "Oh, I just have a little surprise for you. You'll see!"

I groaned in playful annoyance. "Come on, Mom, not even a hint?"

"Absolutely not!" she responded with mock sternness. "You'll just have to wait and see." The conversation shifted, as it often did when talking with Mom. "Have you spoken to Mikey recently? Is he joining us for Christmas?" she asked, her voice tinted with hope and worry.

A pang of guilt tightened around my heart. Mom didn't know Mikey was in rehab. He had pleaded with me not to tell her, wanting to fight his battles privately. Every day was a struggle for him, and I respected his decision, but it made conversations like this challenging.

"Uh, I'm not sure, Mom. You might want to call and ask him," I deflected.

She sighed, disappointment clear in her voice. "I try, darling, but he never answers. Sometimes I feel like he's avoiding me."

"It's not you, Mom," I reassured her, wishing I could say more. "He's just going through some stuff. Give him some time."

Before she could press further, Mom changed the subject, her ADHD-driven enthusiasm steering the conversation to her new garden project. I listened with half an ear, smiling at her typical scattered energy.

As I chatted with my mom, I wandered to the window, pulling aside the curtains to reveal a breathtaking winter scene. The landscape was blanketed in an untouched layer of snow, which sparkled brilliantly under the morning sun. Each tree branch wore a coat of frost, turning them into delicate crystalline structures that glistened like diamonds. The sky was a pure azure, contrasting strikingly with the pristine white below. A sense of peace settled over me, the beauty of the winter wonderland serving as a tranquil backdrop to Mom's familiar voice.

My fingers played absently with a strand of my hair, twirling it around in loops. As we talked, I wandered back to my bed, its softness lulling me into a false sense of timelessness.

"So, darling, how has it been going with your bosses? You were so nervous before leaving. Are they as intimidating as you'd imagined?" Mom asked, the same touch of worry in her voice.

A chuckle escaped me as fleeting memories of the hot tub event swirled in my mind. "It's been... unexpected," I began, carefully choosing my words. "I mean, they're a handful in the best way. The work keeps me on my toes, but they've been kind enough to let me use their hot tub, which has been pretty damn nice."

And that right there was where the information stopped.

"Oh, that sounds divine!" Mom cooed. "You always did love a good soak. I'm glad you're finding moments of relaxation amid all that work. And just think of the extra cash you're pocketing. I *was* thinking of redoing the kitchen, hint hint."

Mom was clearly messing around, but all the same, my heart warmed at the thought of contributing to the house I grew up in. "That'd be great. It's about time that old kitchen got a face lift."

Mom chuckled, "Right? I can't wait. It's long overdue. And maybe with your extra earnings, you can treat yourself a bit. Perhaps a spa day?"

I smiled, visualizing a day of pampering. "God, that'd be amazing. But with my current schedule, the best spa day I'm going to get is a quick dip in the hot tub."

Our conversation took a lighthearted turn, with Mom discussing neighborhood gossip and me sharing some of the lighter, more comedic moments I'd experienced at the cabin. The ease and flow of our talk was something I cherished. Even hundreds of miles apart, it felt like she was right beside me.

However, the tranquility shattered when a quick, anxious glance at my bedside clock made my heart race. "Oh, damn," I whispered sharply.

Concern instantly colored my mother's voice. "What happened? Everything okay?"

Pulling myself upright, panic setting in, I exclaimed, "I overslept, Mom! I usually have breakfast ready by now. I can't believe I let time slip away."

She let out a soft sigh, her decades of motherhood shining through. "Oh, honey. You're always so conscientious. Just remember you need your rest too."

Laughing, albeit a bit nervously, I began gathering my things, preparing mentally for the breakfast rush. "I'll remember that. But for now, I've got to dash. I love you so much, and I'll call you the moment my plane lands, okay?"

With her trademark chuckle, Mom teased, "For the whole twenty-four hours before you're airborne again?"

Grinning, feeling the weight of the morning's urgency but grateful for the bond I shared with my mom, I shot back, "Exactly! Now, I really have to run. Love you, Mom."

The cold sensation of the hardwood floor greeted my feet as I sprang out of bed. Every moment counted now. Scanning the room for something suitable to wear, my attention shifted to the soft, rhythmic knock at the door. I reached for my robe hastily, draped it around me, and swung the door open, half-expecting it to be one of the guys coming to demand breakfast.

To my surprise, it was Isaac, holding a tray laden with a delightful breakfast assortment. The smell of fresh toast and brewed coffee wafted through, making me momentarily forget my earlier embarrassment.

My cheeks burned as I stammered, "I'm so sorry, Isaac. I swear I set my alarm. I must've..."

He silenced my bubbling apologies with a gentle chuckle. His eyes, so often guarded, were soft. "Hey, it's okay," he soothed, "Turns out, Vinnie turned off your alarm. He thought you deserved some extra rest."

I groaned in exasperation. "That man is going to get an earful from me!"

Isaac's laughter was like a melody, calming and gentle. "Honestly, it might've been for the best. You've been working tirelessly since you got here."

"I still have responsibilities," I huffed.

His grin widened and was more confident, showcasing effortless charisma that set him apart from his friends. "Well, right now your only responsibility is to get back into bed and enjoy this breakfast I've got for you."

I raised an eyebrow, the cheek of him demanding such a thing. But his smile was infectious, disarming, and it sent an odd warmth spiraling down my spine. Perhaps it was the genuine care in his gesture, or maybe the allure of the breakfast tray he held. Either way, the combination was too irresistible.

With a dramatic roll of my eyes, I retreated to the bed, settling against the plush pillows. "Fine, but only because you brought food," I teased.

Isaac set the tray down on the bed, its contents meticulously arranged. There were fluffy pancakes, their golden hue promising sweetness, a side of crispy bacon, a pot of freshly brewed coffee, and even a vase with a single rose, its crimson petals vivid against the white porcelain.

"For you," he said softly, pointing to the rose. "Thought it might brighten up your morning."

I was taken aback. It was such a simple gesture, but coming from Isaac, it spoke volumes. This was a side of him I hadn't seen before, and it made my heart flutter in unexpected ways.

"Thank you, Isaac. This means a lot," I whispered, my fingers brushing the cool petals of the rose.

He nodded, his eyes momentarily intense, filled with unspoken thoughts. "You're welcome, Becca. Enjoy your breakfast."

As I began to eat, I couldn't help but reflect on the surprising tenderness of the moment. With these men, every day was an adventure, filled with unexpected moments of warmth, camaraderie, and now, with Isaac's gesture, a hint of something deeper.

CHAPTER 16

ISAAC

The morning after the hot tub escapade, I couldn't shake the feelings of regret and jealousy that had seized me during the night. Vinnie, Archer, and Luke were my lifelines, and as I poured out my frustrations to them, they helped me realize I was sabotaging any chance of happiness out of fear.

Becca was unlike any woman I'd met, and I had to admit it to myself. It was not only her beauty but her spirit, her kindness, that drew me in. But I also knew I'd been hiding from her, shielding myself from any possibility of being hurt again.

So, I decided to take matters into my own hands. That morning, I took up the role of the chef, preparing breakfast for everyone. But for Becca, I took extra care. I whipped up a hearty breakfast and arranged it meticulously on a tray, ready to serve her in bed.

As I walked up the staircase to her room, I felt a surge of anticipation, but also a twinge of nervousness. What would she say? Would she question my sudden change of attitude? I gently knocked on her door and waited.

Her hair was a tousled mess, cascading over her shoulders, and the faintest imprint of the pillow creased her cheek. She seemed momentarily surprised, but then a soft smile spread across her face. Clutching the duvet to her, she made room for me to come in.

I explained why she'd slept in, how it wasn't her fault. Figured a hard worker like her would about die at the idea of missing her duties. I was glad to give her the news.

I'd been all ready to leave her alone to enjoy her breakfast, but as soon as I started out, she stopped me.

"Just FYI, as much as I appreciate the meal, I eat about half the portion sizes as you guys." She smiled, nodding toward the food.

The amount of food on her tray was far more than a woman her size would eat. I laughed. "Force of habit, I suppose."

"Sit," she said. "Help me out with this bacon."

I did as she asked, sitting across from her at the little two-person table near the window. The outdoors shimmered white, and it promised to be a gorgeous day. Becca loaded up a side plate with some bacon and pushed it over to me.

She hesitated for a moment, her fork midway to her mouth. "Why weren't you in the hot tub last night?" she asked, her gaze steady and probing.

For a second, I was taken aback. "Did you see me watching?" I stammered, thinking she might've caught me during my moment of longing.

She chuckled, shaking her head. "No, but you just confirmed my suspicion," she replied with a sly smile.

Despite myself, I laughed. She caught me. "To be honest, I have some baggage. Past mistakes and pains. It made me hesitant to join."

She studied me for a long moment, her fork paused in the air. "You know, we all have our pasts," she began softly. "But every day is a chance for something new."

I nodded, realizing she was right. Maybe it was time for me to let go of my past and embrace the potential future right in front of me. With that thought, the room felt lighter, and I knew I had made the right decision.

The warmth in the room seemed palpable, and I took a deep breath, ready to face my past demons head-on. "There was a woman... Mindy. She was my everything, or so I thought."

She put down her fork and gave me her full attention. "What happened?"

I looked down, taking a moment to gather my thoughts. "She cheated on me with a person I considered a close friend. It was devastating." The pain was still raw, even after all these years, but admitting it out loud felt cathartic.

Becca's expression softened, her gaze filled with empathy. "I'm so sorry, Isaac," she murmured. "That must've been really hard."

I nodded, swallowing the lump in my throat. "It broke me. I closed myself off to the idea of dating or finding love again. My trust was shattered, and I was afraid."

She sat up a bit straighter, her hand reaching out to touch my arm gently. The sensation of her fingers on my skin sent a jolt of electricity through me. "Isaac, I can't even begin to imagine how that felt. But you deserve happiness. You deserve to move on and find love again."

I smirked bitterly. "I've been telling myself that for years. But seeing you, being around you... It's made me question if I'm ready to try again."

Becca's smile was radiant, full of hope and understanding. "We're on vacation, Isaac," she pointed out with a teasing lilt. "Vacation rules apply. We're here to have fun, no strings attached. There's no pressure to define anything."

Her words washed over me, light and freeing. I knew she was right. This was a chance to let go of my inhibitions and simply enjoy the moment. And looking at her, with her inviting eyes and the playful curve of her lips, I felt an undeniable pull.

As if sensing my inner turmoil, she shifted closer, her face tilted up in a clear invitation. My heartbeat quickened. I could feel the warmth of her breath on my face, the promise of softness in her parted lips.

Leaning over the table, I pressed my lips to hers, reveling in the sweetness of the moment. The kiss was gentle at first, a mere brush of lips, but it quickly deepened. It felt like a confession, a pledge, a release. The weight of the past, of Mindy and her betrayal, seemed to lift with every passing second.

My heart raced, drumming in my ears with an intensity that made it hard to focus on anything else. The feel of her lips, soft and inviting, drew me in deeper. Every instinct urged me to be closer to her, to feel more of her. I stood and pulled her up with me, flattening her against me before pressing my lips back to hers.

As the kiss continued, I felt her fingers deftly undoing the buttons of my shirt, tracing the contours of my chest, urging me to shed the barriers remaining between us. With a gentle push, I parted her robe, revealing the softness beneath.

She gasped softly, her brown eyes darkened with desire, staring intently into mine. The curve of her body, the delicate skin, it was all a feast for the senses. My hands glided over her form, admiring the softness, the warmth, the undeniable allure of her.

As I deepened the kiss, she responded with a fervor that matched my own. We were two souls, locked in a dance of passion, both seeking the same thing – to lose ourselves in the moment. With gentle hands, she worked on my belt and trousers, bringing me down to just my underwear. Every touch was electric, every breath shared between us was a testament to the tension building.

Her hand slipped under the waistband of my boxer-briefs, taking hold of my stone-solid cock and stroking it slowly, her fingertips teasing my end. I returned the favor, moving my hand between her thighs and teasing her pussy through the thin, soft fabric of her panties.

Lost in our world, it was easy to forget the surroundings. So when the tray laden with food tipped over, crashing onto the floor and spilling its contents, we both jolted back to reality. I gazed down at the mess, a mix of amusement and regret playing on my face.

"Well, that was unexpected," I remarked, a hint of laughter in my voice.

Becca giggled, her cheeks flushed. "I guess we got carried away."

Before either of us could react further, the door to the room swung open, revealing the familiar faces of the Gallo brothers. Vinnie's eyes widened in surprise, an amused smirk playing on his lips.

"Looks like we missed the breakfast party," he teased.

Archer, ever the gentleman, quickly picked up the over-turned tray, while Luke laughed heartily, "Seems like breakfast in bed took a whole new meaning."

The room was filled with a mix of mirth and tension. Becca adjusted her robe with a cheeky grin. "You guys always have impeccable timing," she quipped.

I ran a hand through my hair, somewhat embarrassed

but mostly amused. "You could've knocked," I pointed out, trying to regain some semblance of composure.

Vinnie winked. "Where's the fun in that?"

Becca giggled, her eyes twinkling with mischief. "Well, since you guys are here, care to join?" she teased, her tone light and playful.

The Gallo brothers shared a look that made it clear they were down.

And despite my previous misgivings, so was I.

CHAPTER 17

VINNIE

From the moment I walked into the room and saw Isaac and Becca tangled up with each other, a heat had spread through me, quick and undeniable. She looked both vulnerable and powerfully alluring, and I couldn't help but appreciate the view, even if Isaac had managed to get there first. The atmosphere was thick with anticipation, but there was also an underlying ease – a comfort we'd built over the past two days.

Luke and Archer seemed equally entranced. We exchanged glances, silently communicating our intentions. It felt both exciting and unnerving. As we began to shed our clothes, down to our underwear, a tension filled the air.

Becca's gaze flitted from one of us to another, her lips curled into a sly, teasing smile. "Well, looks like I'm quite the popular girl today," she purred, her tone dripping with playful sarcasm.

Luke chuckled, his deep voice rumbling with amusement. "You have no idea," he responded, shooting her a sultry look.

Trying to navigate the logistics of the situation, I

remarked, half-jokingly, "So, any preferences on how to start this dance?"

Becca laughed, "How about I leave that to you guys? I trust you to orchestrate."

Luke stepped forward and tugged the robe from her shoulders, allowing it to drop on the floor at her feet, before Becca stepped out of her panties. She lay back on the bed, her body a canvas of curves and softness, waiting for us to paint our desires. Archer positioned himself between her legs, his gaze intense and focused. She shivered in anticipation.

The rest of us found our spots, our touches and caresses mapping her body, ensuring every inch felt appreciated. The room was filled with soft sighs, gentle moans, and the palpable energy of intertwined desires.

There was a beauty in the intimacy we were sharing. It was raw and uninhibited. It was more than just physical; it was about trust, connection, and the thrilling unknown of what lay ahead.

Seeing Archer work his magic on Becca, watching his tongue dancing on the pink, glistening line of her pussy, hearing her gasps and moans, stirred something primitive and raw inside me. It was mesmerizing to watch, and even more so as Becca's wandering hand sought me out, her fingers teasing the waistband of my underwear before venturing further. I felt my body respond almost instantly. The sensation of her fingers around my hardness, coupled with the sight before me, was a heady mix.

As she took me in her hand, our eyes met. A fire burned in her gaze, a challenge, a tease. I couldn't help but smirk. "Enjoying yourself?" I whispered huskily, my voice tinged with the effort of maintaining control.

Becca responded by shifting, bringing her lips dangerously close to me. The sensation of her breath, warm and shaky, sent a shiver down my spine. She took her time, teasing and testing, drawing out every moment until I was practically begging for more. Then she wrapped her lips around me, taking me into her mouth.

I felt every touch, every caress, every flick of her tongue as if it was amplified tenfold. Every sensation seemed heightened, maybe because of the mix of watching and being watched, of being both an observer and an active participant. It was a dance of pleasure, a mix of give and take, of dominance and submission.

Becca's soft grunts signaled Archer's success in his endeavors with her, and I watched with appreciation as her body shuddered in response to his ministrations. The room was thick with the scents and sounds of desire. By the time Luke positioned himself to take his turn, the intensity was almost palpable.

Luke had this way about him – confident, sure. Becca seemed to respond instantly, her body arching, her hands gripping the sheets. He moved with a rhythm that bespoke of experience, his focus entirely on the woman beneath him. The two moved together in a dance as old as time, their bodies finding a rhythm both passionate and tender.

All the while, Becca's attentions on me never wavered. It was exquisite torture, feeling her lips and tongue, hearing her moans. The experience was overwhelming, an overload of senses and emotions.

It wasn't long before I felt the familiar tension coiling tightly inside me, signaling the impending rush of pleasure. I groaned, my hands gripping Becca's head, urging her on. "Becca," I growled, my voice thick with desire.

And then I was gone, lost in a world of sensation and

pleasure. The intensity of the release left me breathless, feeling both drained and invigorated.

The room was filled with the afterglow of our shared passions. It was moments like these that blurred the lines, making distinctions of dominance and submission, of watcher and participant, almost redundant.

There's a particular kind of energy in the room after a shared experience. As I watched Luke and Becca move together, there was an undercurrent of intimacy resonating through the air. Luke, with his relentless charm and finesse, had Becca writhing and moaning beneath him. The sight was almost poetic, the kind that leaves an indelible mark on your mind. Their synchronized release, her scream intertwining with his groan, was a testament to the pleasure shared.

Archer positioned Becca to take her from behind. The change in dynamics was evident, but Becca embraced it, pushing back against him with a fervor only fueled Archer's enthusiasm. He held onto her hips, controlling the rhythm, making sure she felt every single inch of him. His strong, sure thrusts combined with Becca's pleasured sounds made it clear they were both deeply lost in their own world.

When he finally brought Becca to another intense release, it was like witnessing a firework display, bright, passionate, and momentarily blinding.

With the three of us done, the stage was set for Isaac.

The way he looked at Becca was different. While we were playing with pure lust, there was a depth in Isaac's gaze that screamed of longing, of emotions kept under wraps for far too long. His movements were deliberate but tender. He touched her as if she was something precious, something to be cherished.

With every caress, every kiss, Isaac seemed to be

communicating a thousand unspoken words. Words of regret for staying away, of longing for this closeness, of gratitude for this chance. Becca responded to him with equal ardor, her fingers tracing patterns on his back, her eyes locked onto his with an intensity that was both surprising and heartening.

Their rhythm, once established, was a mix of the languid and the frantic. Slow, deep thrusts that spoke of a need to savor the moment combined with moments of unbridled passion, where bodies clashed, lips met, and sounds of pleasure echoed off the walls.

As Isaac and Becca moved together, the rest of us watched in silent appreciation. It was more than just the act. It was the unveiling of a man we thought we knew, revealing a side of him that was as vulnerable as it was passionate.

The crescendo of their shared experience was both visual and auditory. Isaac, his usual composed self lost in the throes of pleasure, his voice a deep baritone of satisfaction. Becca, her entire body a testament to the delight she felt, her voice reaching octaves signaling her sensual release.

Soon we were all laying together, our bodies covered with sweat, content smiles on all of our faces.

Before too long, Becca sat up.

"Hope you guys weren't planning on staying in bed all day – we've got a winter wonderland to explore!"

CHAPTER 18

LUKE

The morning sun peeked through the thick pine canopy, its rays scattering in shimmering patterns across the snow-laden deck of our cabin. As I sat nursing my cup of coffee, I couldn't help but watch the scene unfold before me. Archer and Vinnie were helping Becca prepare for their hike, adjusting straps and making sure she was comfortable with her gear.

There she stood, looking like a winter vision in her snug hiking gear. The muted tones of her clothing contrasted beautifully with the brilliant white world around her. A soft beanie covered her head, stray tendrils of hair escaping, dancing in the cold breeze. Her scarf, a splash of vibrant color against the icy backdrop, flapped gently, while her boots left crisp footprints on the fresh snow.

As they began their trek, a sense of nostalgia washed over me. In just a few days, Becca had weaved magic into all our lives. Her culinary skills had left us all in awe; every meal was an experience, from rich savory dishes to delectable desserts. But it wasn't just her skills in the kitchen that captivated us. The way she captured moments with her camera, freezing time and evoking deep emotions, was unparalleled.

What caught me off guard the most was how she had brought life back into Isaac. The man had built walls so high around himself that laughter seemed a distant memory. But with Becca, even he had found reasons to chuckle.

Becca was an enigma. She had an innate ability to pull you into her world, making everything brighter, louder, and infinitely more enjoyable. Over the past few days, I'd come to realize that what I felt for her wasn't just admiration or infatuation. It was deeper, like roots of an old tree seeking nourishment. I yearned for more than just the fleeting connection of this holiday.

I shook my head, trying to dispel the whirlwind of emotions. Was I being unreasonable? Was it too soon? But then I thought of Archer. We'd always been on the same page about most things. I had a feeling he'd see the potential of what we all, including Becca, could be together. The concept was unconventional, yes, but weren't the best things in life often unexpected?

The speed of it all was dizzying. How do you propose such a unique relationship dynamic? And more importantly, would Becca even consider it? The idea of her being with all of us was certainly not traditional. It demanded understanding, trust, and a level of openness that was rare. But then again, everything about Becca was rare.

I took a deep breath, my misty exhale mingling with the crisp winter air. Below, I could see the trio navigating the trails, their laughter echoing in the vastness, punctuating the serenity of the scene. I thought of the wild horses in the distance, the embodiment of freedom and beauty, and how they mesmerized Becca. In many ways, she was like them – wild, passionate, and free.

The snow continued to fall gently, blanketing the world in a shimmering white layer as I mused on the possibilities of the future. The dynamics of a shared relationship intrigued me, but the risks were undeniable. Vinnie, the optimist as always, might see the potential beauty in it, the sheer exhilaration of exploring something so unconventional and raw. But Isaac?

Isaac was a guarded fortress. The wounds of his past were still fresh, making him cautious and measured in his steps. Just as he had hesitated to join us, this idea might send him into a protective shell. I'd seen glimpses of vulnerability in those deep-set eyes, a fear of loss, of heartbreak. Bringing up a shared relationship with Becca would be playing with fire, but maybe, just maybe, it could be the healing touch he needed.

My thoughts were interrupted by the familiar tune of my ringtone. A glance at the screen showed it was Sal, my Dad. I quickly answered and was instantly hit with a blast of his characteristic enthusiasm.

"Hey, Luke!"

Laughing, I replied, "Hey to you too, Pops. Good to hear your voice."

Dad chuckled on the other end. " So, how's the trip? You boys having fun?"

I smirked, thinking of the escapades of the past week. "It's been... great. Really great," I emphasized, avoiding any revealing details.

A few beats of silence passed, letting me know Dad had something on his mind.

I laughed. "Get to it, old man. You've always been shit at playing coy."

Dad joined me with a laugh of his own. "Fine, fine." His

voice took on a softer tone. "Well, to get right to it, I think it's time you guys finally met Mary."

"Mary, the famous girlfriend our old man's crazy over? You're ready for her to meet your boys?"

He laughed, a tinge of nervousness to the sound. It'd never been easy for Pops to talk about romance, not even with his newest paramour.

"Yep. And she's ready to meet you guys, too."

I grinned. "I'd love to, Pops. We'll be there for Christmas."

"You're in for a treat. Mary... she's a breath of fresh air. And speaking of treats, we have a surprise planned for you on Christmas Eve. Can't say what it is, but I promise, you'll love it."

I raised an eyebrow, intrigued. Dad was never one for surprises. "Now I'm curious."

"What time can I expect you guys?"

Leaning back in the outdoor chair, I replied. "We plan to be there the day before Christmas Eve."

"That'll work perfectly," he said with a chuckle that suggested mischief. "Our surprise will be all set up by then."

Curiosity piqued, I prodded, "What the hell are you going on about, old man?"

Dad's voice was filled with amusement. "No hints, son. Mary and I want to see the genuine reactions on all of your faces. Believe me, it'll be worth the wait."

As much as I wanted to press further, the call ended with our usual farewells and a promise to catch up in a few days. I pocketed my phone and sank into my thoughts, only to be pulled out when the sliding door to the deck creaked open. Isaac ambled out, a ceramic mug clutched in his hand, steam wafting from it. I could just about catch the distinct aroma of scotch.

"The old man on the line?" Isaac queried, taking a sip from his mug.

I nodded, an amused smile playing on my lips. "Yeah. And he's being cryptic about some surprise he and Mary have planned for us on Christmas Eve."

Isaac's brow furrowed, intrigued. "Knowing your pops, it could be anything from a pet monkey to a mariachi band."

We both laughed at the absurd imagery, but it did nothing to quell our shared curiosity.

Peering into the distance, Isaac pointed out, "Looks like they're heading back."

Following his gaze, I saw the silhouette of Becca between Archer and Vinnie, their figures growing clearer as they drew closer to the cabin. Their laughter, carried by the wind, broke the serene stillness of the snowy landscape.

The sight of Becca triggered a fresh wave of contemplation. Taking a deep breath, I finally voiced the question that had been nagging at me. "Isaac, have you thought about what happens when we're back at the office next week?"

He took a long sip from his mug, his face contemplative, eyes trained on the melting snow. "Honestly? No. I've been so lost in the present, the future hasn't really crossed my mind. Which is... weird. It's usually the opposite."

I nodded in understanding. "Same here. This week has been intense, to say the least. But it's also been real. I'm not willing to forget it once we're back to the hustle of city life."

Isaac met my gaze, his expression unreadable. "I get that. But how do you envision things playing out? Especially with Becca?"

I hesitated, carefully choosing my words. "I think there's potential for something more. More than just a fleeting holiday connection. It's unconventional, and there will be challenges, but it's worth exploring."

Isaac looked deep in thought, swirling the remnants of his drink in the mug. "I've never been one for convention," he finally admitted, a hint of a smile forming. "But this... I need to think it through."

As the trio approached the cabin, the weight of our conversation lingered in the air. The future was uncertain, filled with potential complications and risks. But there was no doubt in my mind that it also held the promise of something beautifully unique, something we could share together.

CHAPTER 19

BECCA

The aroma of coffee brewing combined with the sizzle of bacon filled the spacious cabin kitchen. Sunlight poured through the large windows, casting a warm glow over everything, a stark contrast to the cold outside. I whisked eggs, humming softly, but my heart wasn't entirely in the task. It felt as if there was a rock lodged in my chest, a heaviness that came from the impending end of this magical week.

After a restless night, with sleep eluding me at every turn, I'd found comfort in the rhythmic kneading of dough during the early hours. Now, a golden-brown loaf sat cooling on the counter, its crust crackling softly.

The harmonious blend of aromas crafted a sensory symphony, which I hoped would serve as a reminder of the warmth and care I felt for the men I'd grown so close to during our week together.

Each plate I set, each piece of toast I buttered, was a bitter reminder that our time was ticking away. With every dish I prepared, I mentally counted down the hours left. The realization that this was our last morning together, that soon I'd be back in the hustle and bustle of the executive kitchen, felt almost like a physical blow.

I took a moment, leaning against the counter, letting the feelings wash over me. I had fallen. Not for one man, but four. Four men, who in their unique ways had claimed parts of my heart. The reality was surreal. Breakfast was almost ready, and I had something important to say. As the men started filtering downstairs, their heavy footfalls sounding through the house, I mentally prepared myself.

The laughter and voices of the men reached my ears, and I turned to see them entering the living room, making their way to the kitchen. Their smiles, the way their eyes lit up seeing me, warmed my heart. They were unaware of the internal conflict raging inside me.

The soft glow of the morning sun filtered through the kitchen window, illuminating the room in a soft, golden hue. As I stirred my coffee, I mentally practiced the speech I had prepared. Every word was chosen carefully, each sentence crafted meticulously to convey my emotions, my concerns, and my hopes.

I knew the weight of this conversation. The balance of our relationships lay delicately on the fulcrum of what I would say next. My bags were already packed, resting in the trunk of my car, signaling the inevitable end of our week together. I had decided, after I said my piece, I would leave immediately, giving them, and myself, space to process.

I aimed to have four days apart, praying the physical distance would grant me the mental clarity I desperately needed. The way these men affected me, the sheer magnetism of their presence, was almost too much. I needed to know that I could face them in a professional setting without succumbing to the raw desire that seemed to perpetually simmer below the surface.

Isaac was the first to stride into the kitchen, his usual stern demeanor softened by the morning light. As he kissed my cheek, his lips lingering just a moment longer than usual, a flutter of affection and longing stirred in my chest. Vinnie, forever the charmer, followed suit, pressing a gentle kiss to my forehead, his playfulness evident in the twinkle in his eyes. The men said their "good mornings" in their own way, and I cherished each one of them.

Luke and Archer, always the pair, entered together, their presence filling the room in a way that was both commanding and comforting. They each gave me a soft kiss on the lips, a tender gesture that sent my heart racing.

As they went about filling their plates, the familiar camaraderie between them was evident. Their laughter, the inside jokes, the teasing – it was a symphony of love, trust, and friendship. Watching them, a lump formed in my throat and made me question the decision I was about to make.

However, as the weight of their gazes fell on me, the reality of the situation came crashing back. Clearing my throat to gather their attention, I took a deep, steadying breath.

"Guys," I began, my voice surprisingly steady despite the whirlwind of emotions inside, "I need to talk to you."

Four sets of eyes, each reflecting a myriad of emotions, focused on me. The room, moments ago filled with chatter and laughter, fell silent.

"I'm leaving after breakfast," I began, my voice quivering slightly despite my best efforts to maintain composure. "My bags are already packed and in my car."

Archer's face was a picture of confusion. "Why now? We weren't planning to leave until later this afternoon."

Vinnie's usual playful demeanor was replaced with a

look of hurt. "You serious? Why do you want to leave so soon?"

Isaac and Luke remained silent, their eyes usually so expressive, giving nothing away.

Taking a deep breath, I continued, "This week was incredible. More than I could've ever imagined. The moments we shared, the memories we made, I'll cherish them forever. But I need clarity. I need to understand where we go from here. Is it back to business as usual? Do I just resume my role as Chef Becca, nothing more?"

The room was thick with tension, the silence almost deafening. Their eyes darted between each other, exchanging unspoken words. It felt as though they were having a silent conversation, communicating their thoughts, fears, and insecurities without uttering a single word.

I waited, hoping one of them would break the silence, give me a hint, a sign, some assurance about what lay ahead. But none came.

Realizing perhaps they weren't ready to have this conversation, or maybe they didn't have an answer to give, I nodded, trying to mask the sting of their silence. "I understand," I whispered, even though, in truth, I was more confused than ever.

Turning on my heel, I made my way toward the front door. Each step felt heavy, weighed down by the uncertainty of our future and the looming possibility of goodbyes. Just as my hand touched the doorknob, ready to pull it open and step into the cold, uncertain world outside, a voice broke through the heavy silence.

CHAPTER 20

VINNIE

It was as if time slowed when Becca turned toward the exit. An unseen weight pressed on my chest, making it hard to breathe, and a myriad of emotions coursed through me. Regret, longing, fear. It took a few moments for my legs to respond to my brain's scream to move.

She can't just leave like that. The thought gnawed at me.

Propelled by the realization, I stepped forward. "Becca!" I blurted out, cutting through the tension in the room, drawing the attention of everyone. Not waiting for a response or validation from the others, I dashed after her.

"Becca!" My voice echoed as I raced to the door.

Reaching Becca, I took her hand, forcing her to meet my gaze. "Look, I don't know where the others stand, but for me, this week...it was beyond magical. I don't want this to be just a memory, a fleeting moment in time. I want *us*, Becca. I want more."

She looked surprised, her breath hitching, her expressive eyes wide. Before she could respond, Luke and Archer came to a halt behind me, flanking her on either side.

Luke cleared his throat, his deep voice filled with

sincerity. "Becca, this isn't just a vacation fling for me either. There's something here, between all of us, and I'm not ready to let it go."

Archer stepped closer to her, his eyes intense and unwavering. "You've brought a light into our lives that we didn't even realize was missing. I can't imagine going back to how things were before. I want to be with you, in whatever form that takes."

Becca's gaze shifted to Isaac, who remained silent farther behind the group, his face a mask of contemplation. Though he didn't utter a word, I knew him well enough to see the storm of emotions raging within. The hesitancy, the fear of commitment, but also the undeniable longing.

"I can't speak for Isaac," I said, my voice soft but determined, "But I hope you see that the rest of us want this. Whatever this is or will be. We don't want it to end here."

Each one of us held our breath as Becca's eyes flitted between us, sizing up the weight of our words, gauging the depth of our intent. Then, as if a spell broke, the corners of her lips curved upward, revealing a smile so dazzling it threatened to eclipse the sun.

"I have so many questions," she began, her voice trembling just a tad, revealing a vulnerability that made me want to wrap her in my arms. "This...us," she gestured vaguely, encapsulating the five of us in her words, "is uncharted territory. But if you all are willing to try, to find our way through this unconventional path, then so am I."

A collective sigh that mirrored relief and gratitude coursed through the group. One by one, each of the guys stepped forward, holding her in an embrace that seemed to signify a promise, a commitment to the journey.

With all the intensity and raw emotion that had built up inside of me, I pulled her close. Her warmth radiated against my chest, her softness melting into me. "We'll navigate this together," I whispered into her ear, feeling the tickle of her hair against my cheek.

~

It had been a glorious three weeks since returning from the cabin with Becca. We saw each other more often than not, still managing to keep whatever it was we were doing together under wraps. It was difficult at the office, but we were nothing if not consummate professionals.

As Christmas approached and we made plans to see our father, I sensed something was up with Becca. Sitting in Isaac's living room, she looked fidgety, and the guys all seemed to notice.

"What's up beautiful?" Luke asked.

She shook her head, looking unsure how to bring up the subject of what was bothering her.

"Something's obviously on your mind," I chimed in. "Lay it on us."

Becca huffed a sigh. "Look guys, I'm really happy with how things have been going."

"Uh oh, I'm sensing a 'but' here," Archer put in.

"I don't know, I guess I was just wondering how you were all feeling about this?"

Isaac chuckled. "I would have thought it was rather obvious that we've been enjoying ourselves."

"No, I know that, but..." she trailed off.

"Once we're back from Dad's, we'll figure it all out, every step of the way."

Pulling back, she met my gaze with a curious twinkle in her eyes. "You're going to visit your father?"

Luke stepped in with an easy grin. "We're spending a

few days with him for Christmas. We'll be back a couple days after."

She nodded. "I'm headed to see my mom for Christmas. Looking forward to it."

We all nodded, our minds flitting to the realities awaiting us. But as I held her close, one arm securely wrapped around her waist, I knew we had something worth fighting for.

The atmosphere seemed light, despite the undercurrent of serious conversations we needed to have.

"How about we all enjoy the holiday, and when we get back, we can figure all this out," I responded, relief palpable in my voice. Having a set time to discuss everything meant it wasn't an indefinite wait; we were being proactive in giving this relationship, this...whatever it was, a fighting chance.

Isaac chimed in. "How about Sunday evening after we get back at my place? We should all sit together and figure out the details."

"Ah, there he goes," I teased with a smirk, "Always the rule maker, aren't you?"

Laughter echoed around the group, even Isaac's lips twitched into a half-smile. "Someone has to keep you guys in line."

Becca's chuckle added a melodic note to our laughter. "I'll be there, and just so you know," she pointed at each of us, "I'll have my own list of things to discuss. You're not the only ones with terms and conditions."

The comment, lighthearted as it was, held a weight, reminding each of us that Becca was a strong woman with her own set of expectations. It wasn't just about what we wanted or needed; it was a two-way street.

"I need to head out now," she said after a moment,

breaking the brief, contemplative silence. "Still got a bunch of packing to do before I go to my mom's."

The very idea of her leaving made something tighten in my chest. Each of us moved closer, as if on cue. And one by one, we kissed her. My turn came, and I relished every second. The taste of her, the way her lips molded to mine, the faint scent of her perfume threatened to undo me completely.

Pulling back, I murmured, breathless, "I'm half tempted to scoop you up and carry you to the bedroom. One last time before you go."

Archer grunted in agreement. "You're not alone in that, Vin."

Luke simply nodded, his eyes dark with want. But Isaac perhaps made the most impact. He gently ran a finger over Becca's cheek, a simple, intimate gesture, which made her shiver and press closer. The look they exchanged spoke volumes. There was no doubt in my mind that his walls had come down for good, and there would be no putting them back up.

The moment hung heavy, full of the potential for what might come, and the ache of the immediate separation. Becca took a step back, her eyes shiny but full of resolve. "I promise to text as soon as I'm home from my mom's. Be safe, all of you."

We nodded in unison, watching her walk out the door.

The ensuing silence was only broken when Luke let out a deep sigh. "You know, in just a few weeks, she's entrenched herself so deeply into our lives. It feels odd without her already."

Archer nodded, the ever-present mischievous twinkle in his eyes dimmed by the depth of his feelings. "I'm gonna miss her."

Isaac didn't voice his feelings, but the way he was staring into the distance, his jaw clenched, said it all. The connection he felt towards Becca, though not always expressed in words, was unmistakable in his demeanor.

Feeling the weight of the moment and not liking the descent into melancholy, I clapped my hands together, drawing their attention. "Hey! Come on, guys. This isn't some tragic goodbye. She wants to be with us, and we want to be with her. This is just a brief pause, not an ending."

Luke looked over, a grateful smile pulling at his lips. "Leave it to you to always find the silver lining."

"'That's what I'm here for," I said with a chuckle, trying to infuse some levity into the situation. "We're starting something new, something beautiful. It's going to be perfect, you'll see."

Archer smirked, wrapping an arm around my shoulders. "Always the optimist."

Isaac finally spoke, his voice quiet but filled with conviction. "He's right, though. We've got something special, and we'll figure it out. Together."

Together. That word echoed in my mind, encompassing the bond between the four of us, and now, the potential of a life with Becca interwoven with ours. The future, uncertain as it might be, held a promise of something unprecedented and magnificent. And I was more than ready to embrace it.

CHAPTER 21

BECCA

The hum of the city filtered through my closed window. Despite the icy chill in the December air, the familiar sounds of New York provided a comfort I hadn't realized I missed. I stood in my cozy Williamsburg apartment, looking over the freshly developed photos scattered across my kitchen table. Each image captured the wild elegance of the horses against the backdrop of snow-covered mountains, a vivid memory of the days spent in the cabin.

Carefully selecting the best shots, I framed them. They turned out even better than I'd hoped. These frames, now wrapped in shimmering Christmas paper, would be my late gifts to the men. Each present a token, not just of a beautiful sight, but a reminder of the time we spent together, a symbol of the beginning of this potential relationship.

As I taped and tied bows, my mind wandered. How would this even work? I visualized us walking in Central Park. Would we all go together, drawing stares and whispers from onlookers? Would I have private, intimate moments with each of them? Romantic dinners with Isaac, movies with Vinnie, long strolls with Archer, quiet moments with Luke? Or would our relationship be constantly defined by its plurality?

And the intimacy... I blushed just thinking about it. Would it always be all of us together, entwined in passion, or would there be moments where it would be just one-on-one? Those nights in the cabin had been wild and electrifying, but what about the everyday moments?

Pausing for a moment, I walked over to my window, pushing it open a little to breathe in the crisp winter air. New York in December was a sight to behold. The streets below were lined with twinkling lights, lampposts adorned with wreaths. The laughter of children echoed up from the sidewalks, their faces painted with joy and anticipation.

Just a block away, right outside my favorite bodega, a giant illuminated Christmas tree stood tall, its lights reflecting off the snow-covered streets. It was as if the whole city was wrapped up in a warm, festive embrace. In this moment, surrounded by the magic of the city during Christmastime, my worries felt a little lighter.

A sigh escaped my lips. I didn't have the answers. But that's what Sunday was for, right? To sit down and discuss, navigate this complex web we'd somehow found ourselves in.

I shook off my musings and finished wrapping the last frame. As I wrote their names on each package, I allowed myself a small smile. Regardless of the challenges ahead, one thing was clear: I cared about them, deeply. And they cared about me. Whatever path we chose, we would carve it out together.

The shrill noise of my apartment buzzer cut through the air. I stood still for a moment, trying to remember if I had any packages coming – otherwise, I had no idea who could be here. Hesitantly, I stepped over to the intercom.

"Hello?" I took my finger off the button and listened.

"Yo, sis. It's me."

My breath caught in my throat. Mikey. But what the hell was he doing here? He was supposed to be in rehab.

"Come on up."

It wasn't long before a knock sounded at my apartment door, and I hurried over to open it.

My tall, once-vibrant brother now stood on my doorstep, and the evidence of his struggles was clear. He still possessed the chiseled jawline and striking blue eyes reminiscent of our dad, but those eyes had lost their mischievous sparkle. Dark circles shadowed beneath them, and the pale, gaunt skin made it evident that life's battles had worn him down. His once thick brown hair hung limply, a stark contrast to how he always meticulously styled it during our teenage years.

"Mikey?" I whispered, my voice filled with disbelief.

His eyes, which were scanning the floor, slowly lifted to meet mine. "Hey, Becks," he said softly, a hint of his old self peeking through his voice.

"What are you doing here? You're supposed to be in rehab until New Year's," I asked, trying to keep my voice steady and my emotions in check.

Mikey sighed deeply. "I talked to Mom," he began. "She wanted me home for Christmas. Even bought me a ticket." He offered me a small, sad smile. "Said she thinks it'll do me some good to be surrounded by family."

A tinge of anger ran through me. It wasn't her fault, though. Mom had no idea Mikey was in rehab. She thought she was doing something nice. No, my anger was aimed at my brother.

I leaned against the door frame. "I wasn't expecting this,"

I admitted. "But come in." I stepped aside, gesturing toward the living room.

Mikey hesitated for a second, probably noting the hesitation in my tone, then stepped inside, glancing around my apartment. We both knew our reunion wouldn't be easy, but for the moment, I just wanted to believe the brother I once knew was still somewhere inside the person standing in front of me. Anger bubbled up first, a fierce protector against the hurt I had so often felt because of his decisions.

The moment the door was shut I knew I wouldn't be able to keep myself in check for long. "I paid for you to stay in rehab, Mikey. To get clean and stay clean! And you just leave?" My voice trembled with the force of my feelings. My apartment suddenly felt too small, too confining, for the enormity of our situation.

He paused for a moment, his back to me. It was as if I'd let loose in just the way he'd been expecting. After a few beats of silence, he turned around and faced me. Mikey's eyes, already full of a quiet desperation, took on a more pleading look. "Becks, I'm clean, okay? I promise. I won't go near it again. I can't."

I let out a huff, my fingers nervously playing with a loose string on my sweater. "You've said that before. Over and over. And yet here we are."

His voice grew earnest, desperate to convince me. "This time is *different*, alright? They tried different types of therapies, newer methods. I've got tools and strategies now." But even as he said it, there was a subtle shiftiness in his gaze, a slight hesitation in his voice that belied his words. It was the same dance, the same song. A familiar refrain that played every time he came back from rehab.

It was always "different."

I bit the inside of my cheek, my mind racing. There was

no easy solution here, no quick fix. But as frustrated as I was, I couldn't just send him away. He was my brother, and I loved him. Even if he made the same mistake again and again.

"When's your flight?"

He looked relieved at the change of topic. "It's at eleven. Yours?"

"Ten. Different flights, same place. We can go to the airport together then," I conceded.

Mikey nodded, looking down. "Thanks, Becks."

I paused, searching for the right words. "Just promise me something, Mikey," I said slowly. "When we're home, stay away from your old friends, okay? I know your addiction started in high school, and those same people are still there, waiting to pull you back in."

He didn't respond immediately, but when he did, there was a sincerity in his eyes I hadn't seen in years. "I promise. I promise."

The weight of Mikey's words settled heavily between us. His eyes held a desperation I'd seen countless times before, but there also seemed to be an underlying determination. "I swear, Becks, I'll stay home. I won't go anywhere unless it's with you or Mom. I've changed."

A lump formed in my throat. God, how I wanted to believe him. But time and again, he had made similar vows only to shatter them - and my heart - shortly after. "You still have some clothes in the spare room from when you stayed here last," I managed to say, my voice steady.

His eyes misted over. "Thanks," he whispered, his voice cracking.

"And your extra suitcase, it's in the hall closet," I added, pointing toward the corridor.

Before he turned to head to the spare room, Mikey drew

me into a tight embrace, his chin resting on top of my head. I felt the warmth of his body, the slow rhythmic beat of his heart. It was comforting, familiar. But the ghost of our past hung over us like a specter, casting a shadow over the moment.

"Thank you, Becca," he murmured into my hair.

Breaking the hug, he rushed down the hall, leaving me standing in the living room. I leaned against the doorway, taking a deep breath, trying to find some semblance of calm. Every time he came back into my life, he brought chaos with him. I had told him before that I wouldn't keep rescuing him, that I wouldn't let him stay with me anymore. I had to draw a line somewhere. But staring at the hall he'd just vanished down, my resolve wavered. He was my brother. My flesh and blood.

A memory flashed before my eyes: us as children, laughing, playing in the backyard, the world so much simpler then. But those days were long gone, replaced by a reality filled with rehab visits, sleepless nights, and tearful confrontations.

A thought crossed my mind - was this the surprise my mom had been hinting at? She'd been cryptic on the phone, dropping veiled hints about a Christmas miracle. At the time, I thought she meant some sort of gift. But now, I wondered if she meant Mikey's return.

I sighed, closing my eyes for a moment. Maybe this time would be different. Maybe, against all odds, Mikey had finally turned a corner. The mere possibility of it brought a fragile sense of hope to my heart. But I also knew I had to protect myself, to guard myself against potential heartbreak. And that delicate balance between hope and self-preservation would be my tightrope walk in the days to come.

CHAPTER 22

BECCA

The morning sun was peeking through my blinds, painting the room with strokes of gold. It always amazed me how the New York morning could look so peaceful when I knew outside, the streets were already teeming with life. I took a seat by the window, cradling my coffee mug, enjoying the contrast of the warm drink and the cool morning air.

A familiar shuffle of feet disrupted my reverie. Mikey, with his tousled hair and yesterday's clothes, looked like he'd been through the wringer. Sometimes I felt like I didn't recognize this version of him.

"Morning," he mumbled, his voice raspy. His gaze skittered around the kitchen before landing on the neatly wrapped gifts sitting on the table. A hopeful gleam appeared in his eyes. "Hey, is one of those for me?"

I took a long sip, the taste of my freshly brewed coffee bittersweet on my tongue. "Your gift was rehab," I replied. My tone had a bite, but damn, he needed a reality check.

He scowled, dark circles underlining his eyes. "You ratted me out to Mom, didn't you?"

"No," I exhaled, blowing a stray strand of hair out of my face. "But pull another stunt like this, and I will. In a heartbeat."

Mikey's mouth twisted into a grimace. "I'm telling you, it's different now. Can't you just... I dunno, trust me?"

I almost laughed. "Trust you? Mikey, every time I've trusted you, it's like setting myself up for disappointment. The song's the same, and frankly, I'm tired of the dance."

He slouched against the counter, looking so much younger than his years. "Look, Bec... I'm trying. Really trying. Okay?"

I hesitated. A part of me wanted to believe him – that desperate, little sister part of me. But the other, the one that had cleaned up his messes and seen the toll his addiction took, remained skeptical.

The atmosphere grew thick with tension. Outside, a siren wailed, a dog barked, and the distant sounds of New York in the morning filled the silence between us.

Finally, he sighed, a sound heavy with regret. "Gonna finish packing. Flight won't wait for my sorry ass."

I watched him trudge out, his shoulders slouched. It was moments like these when I missed the old Mikey. The one who'd sneak into my room just to steal my candy stash or who'd make up ridiculous bedtime stories just to hear me giggle.

I ordered an Uber and it showed up thirty minutes later, its headlights piercing through the gray morning.

"Come on," I said when it arrived. "Time to go."

Without a word, we made our way out of the apartment and into the chilly air. I focused on the cherry Christmas décor all around us, letting the happiness of the season keep my feelings about Mikey at bay.

My brother kept his eyes fixed on the passing streets,

and I could tell from his clenched jaw he was stewing in his own thoughts. I, too, found myself slipping into a deep well of worry that always seemed to revolve around him.

I shook my head, trying to shove those feelings aside. It was supposed to be a time for joy and reconnection. Not to mention, I had the guys waiting for me when I got back, and every time I thought of them, a warm bubble of happiness and anticipation grew inside. Their faces, their voices, the way they made me feel – I clung to those memories like a lifeline.

We reached LaGuardia, and the buzz of the airport immediately washed over us. Pulling my suitcase from the trunk, I cast a sidelong glance at Mikey. He looked smaller somehow, and despite everything, a pang of concern squeezed my heart.

"Have a good flight," I said, my voice steady despite my fear he'd find trouble to get into once out of my sight.

His eyes met mine, searching for something. Maybe forgiveness, maybe understanding. But I wasn't sure I could give it to him. Not after everything.

"Yeah. See you there, OK?"

"OK."

He grabbed his single carry-on and headed into the airport, soon vanishing into the crowds. I let out a long sigh the moment he was gone, my mind racing.

His list of wrongs was long. The stealing, the nights he didn't come home only to turn up high or hungover the next morning. And then there was that night – the one that still sent chills down my spine – when I walked into my own home to find his dealer lounging on my couch. That terrifying ordeal led me to invest in a Ring system for my apartment, feeling like a hunted animal in my own den.

I remember thinking, "Is this what family is supposed to be?"

It wasn't long before I was on the flight, the hum of the airplane a backdrop to the thoughts spinning in my head as I looked out of the window. Flying had always been a moment of suspended reality for me, a time where the world below seemed both distant and fascinating. One moment we were up above New York, the city looking so small, and the next we were on our way down.

As we began our descent into Maine, the canvas below transformed into a breathtaking panorama of winter wonder. Despite the beauty outside, an uneasiness settled in my stomach.

By the time I found my way out of the arrivals gate, amidst the hustle and bustle, I spotted my mom and someone with her who was tall, broad-shouldered, and radiating raw masculinity. I blinked a couple of times to make sure I wasn't seeing things. He had salt-and-pepper hair that made him look like a real-life George Clooney doppelganger. His deep-set, blue eyes carried stories I bet he'd tell over whiskey and a late-night campfire. There was also a familiarity to him I couldn't quite place.

I jogged over, my bag bouncing on my shoulder. "Hey Mom!"

"Oh, sweetie!" She hugged me for a few seconds before pulling away and looking to the man next to her.

"So, who's your friend?" I asked.

Mom's face was beaming like she'd won the love lottery. She gracefully hooked her arm around his, her eyes twinkling. "Darling, meet Salvatore."

He shot me a grin, all charm and casual confidence. "Please, just Sal. Only your mom insists on calling me Salvatore."

"I just think it sounds so *sexy*," she said with a Cheshire cat smile.

I shook my head, trying to wrap my brain around this twist. "You've got a boyfriend? And in all our endless phone calls, you decided to leave out this tiny detail?"

"Well, you know," Mom shrugged, a coy smile playing on her lips. "I wanted to make it a surprise."

I playfully nudged her. " Sneaky, Mom." But genuinely, my heart swelled. She'd been through so much; she deserved a second shot at happiness. "Okay, this is a pretty epic surprise," I confessed, pulling her into another hug.

When I let her go, Sal extended his hand to me. "It's a pleasure to finally meet you, Becca," he said. "It goes without saying, but your mother's got nothing but good things to say about you."

I took his hand, and once more I was struck by the insane familiarity I felt at his grasp. Somehow, it was like we'd already shaken hands before.

The two of them looked at each other conspiratorially once introductions were over.

I narrowed my eyes, pointing a playful accusatory finger. "Okay, you two, spill it. What's going on?"

Mom giggled, a bubbly, infectious sound. She was like a teenager with her first crush. "Oh, just a teeny tiny surprise."

"I swear, if you're going to tell me you're eloping to Vegas, I might faint right here," I teased.

They erupted into laughter, the sound echoing in the vast airport hall. "No, sweetheart, nothing of that sort. Promise!"

"If this is about Mikey... then spoiler alert. Been there, done that on the way here."

Sal let out a hearty laugh, the kind that drew attention

and infectious smiles from passersby. "No, no, it's not Mikey."

I sighed theatrically. "Fine, I'll play along. But honestly, Mom, if you've got another George Clooney look-alike in hiding, you need to share."

Mom winked, looking mischievous, while Sal wrapped an arm around her, looking like he'd hit the jackpot.

Seeing them like this, so fresh and so in love, warmed my insides. If Sal made her glow like she was, he was okay in my books. We chatted for another hour or so while waiting for my brother's flight to land and I caught sight of him wandering over to us.

I took a deep breath, trying to dispel the frustration gnawing at me as I watched Mikey casually make his way out of the terminal. His minimalist style hadn't changed; just a carry-on slung over one shoulder. I remembered how we used to joke about his ability to pack his whole life into one bag.

Mom's reaction to seeing Mikey was like witnessing a child finding a lost toy. Her face lit up in a way that made her seem years younger. She sprinted, her heels clicking against the tile, and enveloped Mikey in a hug. From where I stood, I felt a pang of irritation. When had they last shared a genuine embrace like this? When was the last time he allowed her such joy?

I watched Mom and Mikey speak, part of me wondering how long it was going to take before he broke her heart again.

Lost in the swirl of my emotions, I almost missed Sal's approach. He moved with a natural ease, yet there was a keen sharpness in his eyes. "You okay over there?" His voice had a gravelly undertone but was surprisingly gentle.

I blinked up at him, my inner turmoil momentarily halted. "Oh, yeah. Why do you ask?"

Sal's intense gaze scanned my face, making me squirm internally. "You've got that 'I'm about to kick someone's ass' look," he noted with a smirk.

I chuckled, but it was edged with irony. "Nah, just tired from working and getting ready for the holidays. But, thanks for noticing."

He continued to scrutinize me, those familiar, although brand new, eyes, studying my every feature. I had to fight the urge to hide.

"You sure?" he asked me, concerned. "We planned lunch, but if you're not up for it..."

Shaking my head with more enthusiasm than I felt, I replied, "Lunch sounds perfect. I could use a good meal. And," I added with a grin, "a chance to interrogate Mom's new man."

He let out a deep laugh that rumbled through his chest. "Oh, I'm ready for it."

I liked this guy already. He was friendly but fearless, and the way he looked at Mom made it clear he was crazy about her.

Yet, as we trailed behind Mom and Mikey, I couldn't help the tension coiling in my stomach. On the outside, Mikey appeared fine, joking and laughing, making plans for the holiday. But I'd been on this roller-coaster with him for too long to be easily deceived by his façade. My trust, once freely given to him, had eroded over time, chipped away by countless betrayals and empty promises. Now I was stuck in this loop of hope and skepticism, always wary, always watching. No matter how desperately I wished things could go back to the way they were, the scars of the past were a constant, looming shadow.

CHAPTER 23

ARCHER

The gentle lurch of the plane touching down pulled me from my reverie. Outside, Maine sprawled in its frozen glory, the trees and fields dusted with the signature frost of winter. I'd always been mesmerized by the sight, and every time we returned, it felt like the first time.

I immediately whipped out my phone, quickly dialing Dad's number. The familiar tone rang in my ear, but there was no answer. *He's probably out, busy with something,* I thought. *Man can't stop working to save his life.*

"We've got the address, right?" I asked.

Luke gave me a quick nod, his fingers flying across his phone screen. "Just sent it to you. Check."

Outside, our car had arrived, the sleek black machine waiting patiently for its passengers. Climbing in, Vinnie could barely contain his enthusiasm. "Looking forward to seeing the old man," he said, his voice echoing my own anticipation. "Though it's a pity about Gia and Guilia not being able to join us. But Italy during the holidays is quite the experience."

The memories of our childhood visits came flooding

back. Cobblestone streets, the echoing laughter of our relatives, and the tantalizing aroma of fresh pasta and sauces.

"We need to head back there soon. I bet Nonna's already sending the evil eye our way for not visiting," I mused.

Vinnie chuckled, his face glowing with mischief. "Remember the last time? She hit you with her wooden spatula."

I laughed at the recollection. "All for stealing a cannoli. But that thing hurt!" I feigned rubbing my arm in remembrance, making Vinnie guffaw even louder.

Luke's voice carried a hint of nostalgia when he said, "Can't believe it's been so many years since we've been back. But you know, Italy's more than just memories. It's a part of who we are."

Vinnie, always ready with a quip, said, "Well, it's a part of three of us at least." He playfully nudged Isaac.

Isaac might not have been blood, but that was only a technicality as far as we were concerned. He'd been around our family long enough to be part of the brood.

Isaac, nonchalant as always, replied, "Hey, I might not be Italian, but I make a mean carbonara."

Portland's coastal charm always had a way of bringing nostalgia, especially during the Christmas season. As our car rounded the corner, I caught the first glimpses of the house. It stood tall and grand, a beautiful blend of Maine's historic architecture with touches of modernity. The stonework was elegant, exuding an old-world charm, and complemented by rich wooden panels.

Christmas had thoroughly kissed every inch of the place. Twinkling fairy lights traced the outline of the large windows, turning them into portals of golden warmth. The grand entrance was framed by two towering fir trees, their branches weighed down with glistening ornaments and soft snow. Crimson ribbons were tied neatly around the white pillars, and on the porch, lanterns illuminated with soft candlelight flickered in the evening breeze. A massive wreath hung on the door, filled with pinecones, red berries, and delicate snowflakes, radiating holiday spirit.

Vinnie's voice broke my trance. "Looks like Dad's new woman went all out, huh?" His eyes sparkled with anticipation. "Nice house, she's got here."

As I gazed at the house, the front door opened with a burst of warmth, revealing our father. His familiar, broad smile stretched across his face, his eyes alight with happiness. Behind him was a woman who could only be the one he'd told us about, her presence a gentle contrast to Dad's exuberance.

"Figli miei!" Dad exclaimed, using the affectionate Italian term for my sons. His arms were spread wide, inviting us into an embrace.

In a flurry of motion, we converged on him. The joy of reunion, the tightening of his grip around each of us, was a testament to the bond we shared. There was nothing quite like a father's embrace; it felt like home, safety, and unconditional love.

Pulling back, he clapped each of us on the back. "Look at you all! Handsome men," he said, beaming with pride. After a few moments, Dad stepped back and gestured to the woman beside him. "Boys, meet Mary."

"It's wonderful to finally meet all of you," Mary said, her voice warm and inviting. "Sal has spoken so much about each one of you."

Luke took Mary's hand and gently kissed it. "The pleasure is all ours. Any woman who can put up with our old man deserves a medal," he joked.

Mary laughed, a melodious sound. "Well, I must say he's been quite the gentleman."

"Only because he's found someone as wonderful as you," Vinnie quipped, a mischievous grin playing on his lips.

Isaac, leaning in, whispered audibly enough for all of us to hear, "Watch out for these two, they're clearly trouble. Welcome to the family."

Everyone laughed, the sound echoing with the joy of reunion.

I stepped forward, offering a genuine smile. "Mary, it's really great to meet you. I think I've seen you somewhere before, though. Do you perhaps work in New York?"

She raised an eyebrow playfully, "Well, maybe you've seen some of my work. I do some photography, mostly freelance."

I nodded. "There it is. No doubt we've seen some of your work."

Still, I couldn't help but wonder if there was more to the familiarity, as strange as the feeling was.

CHAPTER 24

BECCA

"They're here!" Mom's voice rang through the house with an unmistakable note of joy.

My initial response was one of curiosity and a tiny bit of anxiety. When I tiptoed over to the window for a sneaky peek, my heart thudded wildly, all nerves vanishing as raw shock took over.

Oh. My. God!

The world seemed to tilt on its axis as I stared at the scene outside. It wasn't just any family reunion – it was the Gallo brothers, along with Isaac, all embracing the man I'd come to know as Sal. The very same men who'd turned my world upside down and inside out in the most delicious ways.

A jumble of emotions crashed over me like a tidal wave: panic, disbelief, dread, and even a smidge of excitement. The rational part of my brain kept repeating: *This can't be happening.* But there they were. I suddenly realized why Sal had seemed so familiar. Vinnie, Luke, and Archer didn't look exactly like him, but each of the men carried aspects of their father's countenance.

"Hey, Becca," Mikey's voice interrupted my internal meltdown. "Why're you looking all deer-in-headlights?"

I barely heard him, lost in my own whirlwind of thoughts. He came to my side and took a closer look out the window and whistled.

"You kidding me? Four dudes? God, I hate meeting new people." Without waiting for me to respond, he gave a half-smirk, half-sigh and ambled toward the front door. "Might as well get this meet and greet out of the way. Come on."

As I watched Mikey go, my mind raced a mile a minute. What was I supposed to do? All our secrets were now at risk of being discovered. The layers of complexity to our situation just skyrocketed.

Gathering all the courage I could muster, I decided I'd rather face the situation head-on than cower behind a closed door. Taking one last look in the mirror, I braced myself, put on what I hoped was a neutral, friendly face, and stepped out of the room and down the stairs. My stomach tied into knots as I reached the ground floor.

The men looked impossibly handsome, of course, the four of them slipping out of their coats and gloves to reveal huge, powerful bodies clad in flannel and denim.

Isaac's gaze was the first to find me. Those deep-set eyes frowned in confusion and disbelief. But before the weight of his stare could completely pin me to the ground, Vinnie's gasp yanked my attention his way.

His eyes – always so animated and cheeky – were huge saucers. The shock in them was palpable, as if he'd seen a ghost. And speaking of ghostly, the cold feeling of dread that had settled in my stomach didn't abate when the twins turned my way. They looked so much like Sal in that moment, the resemblance was eerie. Their handsome faces bore identical expressions of surprise, eyebrows raised and mouths slightly open.

The thick silence in the room felt heavy, each second stretching into an eternity. The tension in the air was so thick, I could almost hear my own heartbeat echoing loudly in my ears until Luke broke the silence, a soft chuckle escaping him.

"So, is this our big surprise?" His voice held a hint of amusement, but I could sense an underlying confusion.

Mom, being the ever-bubbly and loving presence she was, burst into a fit of giggles, dispelling some of the tension. She reached for my arm, her grip warm and reassuring. "Surprise indeed!" She laughed, pulling me forward into the group. "Look, Becca – it's your bosses!"

"They sure are!" I said, my voice higher than usual. "My bosses!"

"What an unexpected surprise, Chef," Vinnie said, trying to match my tone.

Everyone was trying to process the surreal situation, and I could feel all their eyes on me. My face heated up, I'm sure turning a lovely shade of lobster-red. Being the center of attention, especially under these circumstances, wasn't my favorite position.

Despite the mind-bending surprise, Vinnie shot me a small, lopsided grin, trying to break the ice. Archer cleared his throat, offering a nod in acknowledgment. Isaac just kept studying me, his gaze intense. And Luke? Well, he still looked faintly amused, a smirk playing on his lips.

The realization hit me then – there was no going back from this moment. My two worlds had just smashed into one another. Nowhere to go but through.

Taking a deep breath, I tried to marshal my thoughts.

Something else occurred to me – Mikey wasn't there. Where he'd gone, I had no idea.

Mom's words filled the tense air. She could definitely sense that something was amiss, even if her understanding of the situation was only partial.

"Okay, look, when I met Sal and finally put two and two together, realizing he's the father of your bosses, I was concerned at first. I mean, come on! What are the odds?" She glanced around and went on. "Sal and I got to talking and, well, while we agreed this complicated things, it was no reason to put a stop to true love, right?"

"That's right," Sal said warmly. Despite the tension in the air, Sal was just as cool and calm as ever. I saw where the brothers got their unflappability from.

It complicated things – those were Mom's words. She didn't know the half of it.

Isaac shifted, his posture slightly stiff. "Well, isn't this a wild coincidence?" he said, though the strain in his voice was evident.

But Vinnie, always the one to step in and lighten the mood, moved forward, wrapping an arm around me in a friendly side-hug. "You know what? This is just plain crazy, but it's fun, right?" The warmth of his hug and the confident tone of his voice were soothing. I leaned into the gesture, and a soft chuckle escaped me. "Our favorite employee's mom is dating our dad. Kind of perfect, really."

"Seriously, out of all the men in the world, my mom decides to date your dad?" I teased, letting out a genuine laugh. It felt good, relieving some of the tension in my chest.

Not one to be left out, Luke approached and held out his arms, pulling me into a warm embrace. "Well, I guess our families were just destined to be intertwined," he whispered, his breath tickling my ear. He then released me, giving my hand a reassuring squeeze. That simple gesture spoke volumes. It was his way of saying, 'We'll get through this.'

I hugged Isaac next, feeling the rigidity in his frame. His embrace was brief but comforting in its own way. And Archer pulled me close. His hug was tight, as if trying to convey all his emotions without words.

Pulling away, I looked at each one of them. "I know this is a lot to process. Hell, it's a lot for me too!" I admitted with a laugh, my gaze flitting to each face. "But let's celebrate, right? True love is in the air!"

The warm looks on Sal and Mom's faces let me know they were pleased with my attitude.

However, despite the fading awkwardness, I couldn't help but wonder what would happen when the other shoe fell. And I had no doubt at all it was going to fall – *hard*.

CHAPTER 25

ISAAC

I t was disorienting, the juxtaposition of her presence against the backdrop of the unexpected revelation. My initial, fleeting thought was an appreciation of Becca's beauty, the way her hair cascaded down her shoulders, the vibrant hue of her eyes that always seemed to pierce straight through me. Two days away from her had felt like a minor eternity. But the serenity of that thought was immediately disrupted by the chaotic realization of the situation.

How was it that none of us knew? The irony of the entire situation was not lost on me. Four men, all connected to Becca, none of us aware that the woman we were falling for was connected to the Gallo boys' father's new flame. And the fact that we, particularly I, who prided myself on being well-informed and in control, had been blindsided? It was both frustrating and humbling.

Mary, ever the gracious hostess, seemed oblivious to the undercurrent of tension in the room. "Come along," she beckoned, leading the way to the dining room. "You all must be starving."

Sal followed her with a wistful glance back at us, obviously sensing the strange dynamics at play. Once the pair was out of the room, I hurried over to Becca.

She was taking it somewhat hard, her expressive eyes a little too wide, a slightly manic undertone to the laughter that bubbled up from her. It was out of character, a kind of nervous laughter that echoed the shared absurdity of the situation.

I took a step closer, my voice a low rumble. "Hey - deep breaths." It wasn't just advice for her; it was a mantra I was repeating to myself. Despite the world seemingly shifting beneath our feet, one thing remained a constant – my attraction to her and the unspoken bond we shared.

She tried to stifle her laugh, covering her mouth with her hand. "Isaac, of all the crazy twists in the world," she whispered, still giggling. "This has got to be the most unexpected."

"I won't argue with that," I replied, offering a small, reassuring smile. I reached out, taking her hand in mine. The touch was grounding for both of us.

The room began to fill with the aroma of the impending meal, the fragrances acting as a momentary distraction. But even as Sal and Mary's food was laid out and we all tried to engage in normal dinner conversation, there was a lingering sense of wonderment, a series of unanswered questions.

As we stood together, a tall figure appeared at the entrance of the dining room. My gaze shifted to the newcomer. His build was lean and a bit wiry. His dark hair, almost the same shade as Becca's but with a hint of a wave, was slicked back, and his penetrating eyes scanned the room, lingering particularly on Becca and the four of us.

I couldn't say for certain, but it seemed as if he was piecing something together, the contemplative expression giving away his intrigue. There was an unmistakable protective aura about him that spoke of countless shared memories and secrets with Becca.

"So," he said, his tone skeptical. "These are the guys, huh?"

"Guys, this is Michael, my brother," Becca interjected, breaking the brief tension. "Michael, these are my bosses—the Gallo brothers: Archer, Luke, Vinnie," she gestured to each in turn, "and this is Isaac Tyson."

"Come on, sis – no one calls me Michael. It's Mikey."

He shook our hands, one after the other, his gaze flicking to each of us. There was a nervousness to him, though he kept an easy smile on his face.

"So, these are the famous bosses, huh?"

"Pleased to meet you," I replied as we shook hands, his palm cool and a bit clammy.

Feeling a sudden need for space, or maybe just something to do, Becca pulled away. "Drinks?" she suggested, a forced cheer in her voice, her eyes darting nervously.

"I'd love a scotch," Sal's voice boomed in from the kitchen. The mention of alcohol seemed to cut through the fog of Archer's surprise, his face brightening momentarily at the prospect of wine.

We all gave our drink orders, though the mention of alcohol seemed to make Mikey a bit skittish.

"I'll go help Mom," he said. He didn't wait for a reply before ducking out of the room and into the kitchen.

Joining Becca at the bar, I helped her pour the drinks, our hands occasionally brushing against each other. "So," I began, opting for a light tone, "how did you miss the memo about your mom dating a Gallo?"

She sighed, "Honestly? She'd mentioned dating someone, but nothing serious. And never a name. Had I known..."

As the door swung open, Mary entered the room, holding herself with the confidence of a queen and the grace of a ballet dancer. Balancing a hefty bowl filled with a salad that boasted an array of colors, she attempted to reclaim the atmosphere. The room, however, was thick with tension, a tangible fog of unsaid words and emotions.

"This was quite the shock," I said with a smile. "Have to admit."

Mary, in a genuine bubbly manner, exclaimed, "Well, Sal and I just thought it'd be the most delightful surprise for everyone. A sort of early Christmas present." She looked around, her eyes scanning each face, hoping to find some signs of agreement, if not enthusiasm.

Becca's response came in the form of another laugh. But unlike her genuine chuckles I'd heard before, this one was different. It was like listening to a melody played on an out-of-tune instrument.

Mary, her motherly instincts immediately kicking in, addressed her daughter's discomfort. "Honey, are you okay?" The concern in her eyes was evident.

Becca, attempting to keep the atmosphere light, replied with a somewhat shaky voice, "I'm absolutely fine, Mom. This... it's just... a hell of a surprise, you know?"

Vinnie, always ready to lighten a heavy room, decided it was his turn to chime in. Flashing a boyish grin, he remarked, "Well, Mary, you've certainly given us a surprise. But, in all honesty, it's a good kind of unexpected."

However, Mikey's approach was starkly different. There was a slight edge to his voice as he commented. "I didn't even realize you were seeing someone." The underlying accusation was palpable. "Why didn't you tell me?"

Mary lifted an eyebrow at her son but said nothing about his tone. Clearly, she didn't want to make a scene. She busied herself, placing the salad on the table, expertly arranging the rest of the dinnerware. "You and I discussed this at the airport, Mikey. Besides, I wanted to make sure this was something serious before I shared the news. And now that I know for sure it is, here we are!"

Seizing the moment to engage Mikey and perhaps diffuse the brewing storm, I ventured, "Mikey, care for a drink?"

But before the words could fully leave my lips, Becca interjected, her voice firm, "He's sticking to water."

The atmosphere grew even more charged. Mikey's eyes shot daggers at Becca. The irritation, clear in the hard line of his lips and the tight clench of his jaw, made me curious. But he refrained from voicing his thoughts. He simply lifted his water glass, the movement slow and deliberate, and drank, eyes locked with Becca's.

It was becoming evident that the undercurrents in this room weren't solely about the surprise coupling of Sal and Mary. The dynamic between Becca and Mikey was intricate, layered. Whatever history they shared, it was certainly complex.

Through the hushed conversations and low hum of excitement, I was momentarily pulled from my observations of the room when Sal entered, balancing a massive pan of his famous lasagna. The aroma filled the room almost instantly with the inviting scent of tomatoes, cheese, and freshly baked pasta. My mouth watered in anticipation.

Becca, maybe searching for some semblance of normalcy in the whirlwind of surprises, noted, "Is this a new table?"

"Oh, isn't it nice?" Mary asked, placing her hand on the smooth wood top. "Picked it up at an estate sale. Well, I *bought it* – big, strong Sal here was the one who literally picked it up and carried it in." She laughed at her joke, Sal smiling and squeezing her arm.

Sal smiled. "It's an antique – and handmade, as far as I can tell. And fitting, too. Big table for a big family."

A glance exchanged between Sal and Mary spoke a thousand words. Their smiles, a dance of shared secrets and silent conversations, made the room feel warmer. The glances I shared with the brothers were more of the curious kind.

With everyone settled and dishes served, Sal lifted his glass, signaling a call to attention. The room grew silent, all eyes on him.

"'To family," he began, his voice deep and resonant as he used that word again. "To unexpected meetings, to reunions, and the moments that bring us closer together. As the year comes to an end, I am reminded of the importance of cherishing every moment, every connection, and every shared laugh. To the ties that bind, and to the future that awaits."

As his words filled the room, my eyes inadvertently found Becca's. There was an unspoken understanding, a silent conversation that seemed to echo Sal's sentiments. Yes, this gathering was about more than just a holiday reunion.

The murmured cheers following the toast were warm, filled with genuine appreciation for Sal's heartfelt words. But before anyone could dive back into their meal, Sal had yet another surprise up his sleeve.

Clearing his throat, a twinkle in his eye, he reached for Mary's hand, urging her to stand. Together, they looked like two teenagers in love, the world around them fading away.

"There's more news we'd like to share," he started, causing an anticipatory hush to descend upon the room. "Mary and I are getting married!"

CHAPTER 26

BECCA

The moment after Sal's proclamation stretched out, time elongating in a cruel trick of reality. As I glanced around, taking in the facial expressions of everyone seated, it felt like the universe was playing the world's worst joke on me. My gaze settled on my mother's glowing face, and my stomach did a visceral flip. Oh, boy, if I managed to keep down those two measly bites of lasagna now, it would be a sheer miracle.

The silence was heavy, punctuated only by the clinking of silverware being set down. Everyone seemed to be in a state of shock. I darted a glance toward Vinnie, expecting him to break the tension. But even he appeared to be momentarily lost for words, eyes wide and mouth agape.

Summoning every bit of acting prowess I didn't know I had, I pasted on the brightest, fakest smile I could muster. "Oh my God, Mom!" I exclaimed, leaping up from my chair. I enveloped her in a hug, doing my best to communicate my happiness and support even if my insides felt like they were staging a violent revolt.

Whispering close to her ear, I tried to find the sincerity in my words, "I'm so happy for you."

Pulling away, I caught her watery eyes, filled with a mixture of happiness and uncertainty, probably gauging my reaction. My mom had been on her own for years, bearing the weight of loneliness, especially with Mikey and me living miles away. The least I could do was be happy for her.

Luke, picking up on my lead -or maybe he just felt the need to save the moment too-, got up and clapped Sal on the back. "Congrats, Dad. Quite the bomb to drop on us, but then again, you've always been full of surprises."

The room slowly erupted into a mix of laughter, congratulatory pats, and shared whispers. I took a moment to breathe, slipping back into my seat.

Vinnie finally piped up. "Well, I guess we're going to be one big, happy family then. Christmas is going to be wild!"

I snorted. "Understatement of the year," I mumbled under my breath, catching Isaac's smirk from across the table.

Archer raised his glass in a toast, "To the unexpected turns in life, and to finding happiness, no matter how unconventional."

I clinked my glass against his, our eyes meeting briefly. "Hear, hear," I whispered, taking a long sip of my wine.

The atmosphere in the room shifted from stunned surprise to warmth, the way fog lifts to reveal a sunny day. A cacophony of "congratulations" and the clinking of glasses echoed as everyone attempted to process the unexpected news. Drinks were poured with a little more enthusiasm, laughter rang a bit louder, and the mood lightened as the reality of Mom and Sal's announcement set in.

As my mother basked in the glow of attention and well-wishes, I stole glances at the men who had come to mean so much to me. Archer met my gaze with a calm that was both reassuring and infuriating. Did nothing phase him? His eyes conveyed a quiet understanding, as if silently promising we'd navigate through this new twist.

Vinnie, being Vinnie, laughed heartily, clinking glasses with everyone, even going so far as to propose a humorous toast. "To unexpected family reunions! May we never run out of surprises... or wine." He winked, eliciting chuckles from the group.

But it was Isaac and Luke whose reactions tugged at my heartstrings the most. Isaac had an edge of discomfort, like a man trying to fit into a suit two sizes too small. His eyes darted away when they met mine, as if pushing back emotions he wasn't ready to confront. Sal may not have been his biological father, but Sal and my mom being married would make our relationship just as complicated as it would with the others.

And then there was Luke. Sweet, protective Luke. Concern was etched across his face, like he was trying to solve a puzzle with missing pieces. I could almost see the gears turning in his head, processing not just the surprise engagement but also its implications for our tangled relationship.

I turned my attention back to the festivities, trying to keep my mind from wandering to the inevitable complications this union would bring. For now, my mom was happy, and that was what mattered.

Mikey had remained aloof, watching as if he wasn't a part of the scene. When he did speak, he sounded as if this were just one more thing messing up his life. "Four brothers...not exactly what I pictured."

"What do you mean?"

"I mean, I always thought Mom would find a guy, but not one with so many kids." He shook his head as if disgusted.

"Just be nice," I warned him. "It doesn't matter if you don't like it. This is about Mom and her happiness."

"Whatever." He lapsed into silence.

Sal, unflappable as he'd been since I'd arrived, though I didn't think he'd overheard my conversation with Mikey, began sharing stories of his courtship with Mom, each anecdote funnier than the last. Mom blushed but laughed along, her hand firmly in his.

I leaned into the laughter, the joy, and the temporary escape from reality. But in quieter moments, when the laughter faded and conversations dwindled to murmurs, my thoughts circled back to my own happiness. Could I celebrate my mom's newfound love while potentially sacrificing my own? The weight of that question, of what lay ahead, threatened to overwhelm me.

Pushing those feelings aside, I refocused on the present. One crisis at a time, I reminded myself. Right now, it was about toasts, smiles, and the joining of two families.

The morning after the big announcement, I was burrowed under the covers, wishing the world away. My alarm had long gone off, its blaring insistence piercing the peaceful morning. With a grunt of frustration, I silenced it and gave into the comforting allure of the blankets.

If Mom and Sal tied the knot, where did that leave me and Isaac and the Gallo boys? The thought looped in my mind. We were already navigating the complicated waters of potential polyamory, but adding the layer of three of them becoming my stepbrothers? That was a twist I hadn't seen coming. And while society had its judgments that I couldn't care less about, this was a line even I hesitated to cross.

Lying there, I could feel the steady thrum of my heartbeat, a rhythmic reminder of the emotions swirling within. It's a bizarre feeling, knowing your heart and mind were at odds. My heart, the hopeless romantic, whispered of love, connection, and the promise of a unique bond. My head, always pragmatic, scoffed at the impossibility of it all.

Deciding that lying around wasn't going to solve anything, I pushed myself up and padded to the bathroom. The cool tiles felt good against my feet, and the familiar surroundings of Mom's home offered a brief moment of comfort. I turned on the shower, letting the water heat up as I undressed. The steam began to cloud the mirror, and I stepped in, letting the warm droplets cascade over me.

The sensation of the water always had a way of making me lose myself, and in no time, I was back to those all-consuming thoughts of the guys. The laughter, the warmth, the chemistry – it was intoxicating. As the water sluiced down my body, my mind began to drift to scenarios best left for private moments. The stolen glances with Vinnie, the intense conversations with Isaac, the playful teasing from Luke, and the undeniable connection with Archer. The scenes played out vividly, pulling me deeper into fantasy.

But with a shake of my head, I forced myself back to reality. Fantasies were one thing, but the reality was far more convoluted. The water was beginning to run cold, a not-so-subtle hint from the universe that it was time to step out and face the day.

A soft knock interrupted my thoughts as I threw on my clothes, and I turned to see my mother's head peeking through the slightly ajar door. Her blue eyes, so much like mine, scanned my face with a mix of concern and amusement. "Goodness, Beck, it's almost noon! You never sleep this late. Everything okay?"

Rubbing my temples, I attempted a reassuring smile. "Just been really busy lately, Mom. Caught up to me, I guess."

She stepped into the room, her delicate floral perfume wafting toward me. Closing the door gently behind her, she took a seat on the edge of my bed. "Honey, I noticed you were a little out of sorts last night. Are you... okay with everything? With Sal and me?"

I hesitated, choosing my words carefully. "It was a surprise, to say the least. But if you're happy, Mom, that's all that matters."

Her face softened, a grateful smile curving her lips. "Thank you. It means a lot. And the boys? I know you still have to work with them. It had to have been very unexpected."

I chuckled, pushing a strand of hair behind my ear. "Tell me about it. I mean, I knew Sal looked familiar. But the fact that your new beau is the father of three of my bosses? That's next level."

Mary tilted her head, her expression curious. "Are they good to you?"

I nodded, recalling the many moments of laughter, camaraderie, and genuine connection I'd shared with the Gallo brothers. I couldn't tell Mom about any of that, of course. "Yes, they're great bosses. Really great."

She smiled, patting my hand. "There's a sparkle in your eyes when you talk about them. I can tell you really love this job, love working for those guys." She pursed her lips and looked away, and I could sense there was something more on her mind. "And I wish this could just be all about cele-brating. But there's something else. Mikey? He's been a little distant. I'm worried about him."

I couldn't tell Mom about Mikey's recent troubles. For all she knew, Mikey's issues were in the past.

My chest tightened. "Yeah, I've noticed. I'm not sure what's going on. But we'll talk, okay? Promise."

Her gaze lingered on me for a moment, as if searching for more answers. But then she brightened, her eyes twin-kling with mischief. "So, after Christmas, will you help me search for a wedding dress?"

I blinked, caught off guard. "Oh, yeah, ok that sounds good."

She nodded enthusiastically. "And you'll need a maid of honor dress as well."

I couldn't help but laugh. The absurdity of it all—the shocking announcements, the unexpected connections—yet there we were, planning a wedding. The world worked in mysterious ways.

Leaning in, I hugged her tightly. "Sounds like a plan, Mom."

She squeezed my hand, her eyes shimmering with tears of happiness. "Thank you, Beck. For everything."

As she wandered out of my room, I shook my head in disbelief. Life was full of surprises, and while some were more challenging than others, moments like these, with love, laughter, and the promise of new beginnings, made it all worth it.

CHAPTER 27

BECCA

Mom's happiness was almost tangible, but beneath the surface, my emotions were chaotic. Marrying Sal, for her, meant a new chapter, a new beginning. For me, it opened a can of complicated, messy worms with Isaac and the Gallo brothers. I felt like I was standing on the edge of a precipice, the ground rapidly eroding beneath me.

Suddenly, I felt exhausted, as if all the wind had been knocked out of my sails. "I know we have guests and all but would you mind if I stayed in my room for a bit? I'm awfully tired all of a sudden."

My mom regarded me with concern, reaching out to feel my forehead. "You don't feel warm."

"No, I don't think I'm sick, I just think work and the holidays and everything is just catching up to me."

"Do I need to have a discussion with those men downstairs about riding you too hard?" she asked, pretending to be stern.

I nearly choked. *If she only knew.*

"No, Mom, you don't need to give them a talking too. I

push myself harder than anyone else ever could, you know that."

"Okay, well, you just settle back in, and if you need anything you let me know, alright?"

"Thanks, Mom," I murmured, appreciating her efforts. "Maybe some rest will sort me out."

She took a step toward the door but hesitated. "How about some soup?" Her voice was soft, layered with maternal concern.

I managed a smile. "Maybe later. I think I just want to close my eyes for a bit now."

She nodded, moving to the door. "Alright, love. Shout if you need anything." She blew me a kiss and left the room, her soft footsteps echoing down the hallway.

The room was dim, sunlight filtering through the curtains casting a muted glow. I adjusted my pillow, sinking deeper into the plush mattress, welcoming it's comforting embrace. As I closed my eyes, my mind began to wander.

My thoughts, as always, veered to the four of them: Isaac, Luke, Archer, and Vinnie. Each of them was a world unto themselves, yet they had become entwined with mine in a way I'd never anticipated. It wasn't just about passion, though there was plenty of that. It was the small moments, the quiet conversations, the shared laughter, and yes, even the complications that connected me to them.

And now, with this unforeseen twist – Sal and Mom, seriously? – everything seemed even more complex. Dating one's stepbrothers was definitely not something I'd ever expected to consider.

Could we navigate this new challenge without losing what we'd built? Or was this an insurmountable obstacle?

The weight of my eyelids became too much, and I felt myself slipping into the embrace of sleep. As I drifted off, I clung to one hopeful thought: if our bond was genuine, if what we felt was real, then we'd find a way. No matter how twisted the path became, fate would guide us through.

~

The quiet knock startled me from the Netflix-induced stupor I'd fallen into after my nap. I shuffled to the door and opened it. There they stood. All four of them, in all their glorious, concerned masculinity.

Isaac cleared his throat. "Everyone's out. Your mom, Sal, even Mikey," he explained, pausing briefly. "So, we thought we'd check on you."

As the guys walked into my room, the warmth and familiarity of our shared connections wrapped around me. I couldn't believe how much my life had changed in just a few weeks. These men, whom I'd known professionally for so long, were now... what? Boyfriends? Complicated stepbrother figures? I didn't have the answer, and from the looks of it, neither did they.

We settled onto the bed, and I noticed Vinnie giving me a concerned look. "You're glowing," he commented, his voice teasing, yet there was a hint of curiosity underneath.

"Yeah," I shot back with a mock roll of my eyes, "it's called sweat. A new beauty regime I'm trying. You should give it a shot."

Luke chuckled, leaning over to squeeze my knee gently. "Glad you're feeling better. We were worried."

Archer, always the perceptive one, caught the fleeting look of confusion in my eyes. "What's on your mind?" he prodded.

I hesitated for a moment, then sighed. "Just... you know,

the usual. Life, weird coincidences, the possibility of becoming a cliché in a soap opera."

Lying down on the plush bed, I heard the rustle of the guys moving about. Archer, Mr. Take-Charge, looked down at me, his eyes filled with concern.

"Maybe you should rest a little more," he suggested, gently pushing my shoulder down when I tried to sit up.

I swatted his hand away playfully. "I promise, Archer, I'm good. Just a weird day," I replied.

The room was thick with tension, each of us lost in our own whirlwind of thoughts. Then Luke, ever the mediator, took a deep breath. "Alright, enough of the awkward silence. We need to address the giant, sequined elephant in the room."

I chuckled, grateful for the break in tension. "You're right. We can't tiptoe around this," I admitted, sitting up straighter. "It's complicated. Like, next-level telenovela complicated."

The guys looked at me, a mix of amusement and seriousness in their eyes. "I've had time to think, and I believe we could try this—whatever this is," I continued, taking a deep breath. "But we have to be on the same page. No secrets, no weird family drama, and most importantly, open communication."

Archer nodded, running a hand over his freshly shaved head. "I'm in. But we have to do it right."

Vinnie flashed one of his trademark grins. "I'm all in, as long as we can still have fun." His statement brought a few chuckles, but he quickly turned serious. "I mean, this is new territory for all of us. We should navigate it with care, but also not lose, you know, the joy and spontaneity."

Isaac, quiet until now, finally chimed in. "I've never

been one to shy away from uncharted territories. We'll figure it out, one step at a time."

Luke, squeezing my hand, added, "Life throws curve balls, and while this situation is unconventional, it doesn't mean we can't make it work. We've faced bigger challenges. Together, we can handle anything."

With a newfound determination, I said, "Alright then, gentlemen. Let's navigate this minefield. And, just so you know, I'm holding each of you personally responsible if we all get blown up in the process." They laughed.

Feeling a tangle of emotions, I took a steadying breath. "Okay, let me just lay it out there. I'm genuinely feeling things I never imagined I could feel for not one, but all of you. Sounds like I'm straight out of some wild rom com, doesn't it? But it's the honest truth. Now with Mom and Sal in the mix, it's..."

Vinnie waved his hands in dismissal. "Becca, we get it, it's complex. But guess what? We're all aboard this crazy train with you. Feelings aren't predictable. They're messy, wild, and at times, downright nonsensical."

His words struck a chord, but I still couldn't shake off the uncertainty completely. The tension in the room was discernible, and as I glanced at each of their faces, I saw mirrored reflections of my own apprehensions and hopes.

Isaac nodded thoughtfully. "Life can be unpredictable. But we've got this, or we'll figure it out. The Mary and Sal situation? It's just another thing we need to figure out."

"Mr. Optimistic," I replied, reaching over and giving his leg a squeeze. "I like it."

Archer's fingers softly traced the outline of my jaw. His voice, deep and resonant, murmured reassurances, "The world's definitions of relationships don't get to dictate our reality."

Luke merely tightened his grip around my hand, his eyes locking onto mine, saying everything words couldn't.

I was certain we were about to kiss. And sitting on my bed, surrounded by the guys, was exactly what I wanted. I closed my eyes and lips began to find my skin – one pair, then another, then another, then another.

"We can't do this right now," I murmured, my eyes still closed.

"Now's the best time, actually," Archer said. "No one here to walk in on us."

Their lips met mine in succession, setting off a series of emotional fireworks. Each kiss, unique in its passion, made my heart race and skin tingle.

Chuckling, I tried to cut through the intensity. "So, you all keep saying we're alone, but are we sure? Like, a hundred percent?"

Vinnie flashed his cheeky grin, his eyes glinting with mischief. "Scout's honor. We have the entire place to ourselves. No interruptions. No unexpected visitors."

My eyebrows arched playfully, "Well then, I hope you guys are ready for some fun. Because believe me, this is what I've been needing since this morning."

Every heartbeat and breath amplified to a deafening level. As I felt Luke's soft lips brush against the corner of my mouth, I was immediately pulled into a haze of warmth. His hands traced patterns on my back, sending shivers down my spine. His kiss was soft and gentle, like the brush of a feather, but it stirred something deep within me, awakening a passion I'd barely tapped into.

Next came Vinnie. His kiss was entirely different, assertive and confident. He took my lower lip between his, sucking gently. The feel of his strong hands framing my face and the soft rasp of his stubble sent a shock of electricity straight to my core. The world around us seemed to blur, focusing only on the rhythm of our breaths and the urgent need building up.

Isaac's approach was delicate, almost tentative. He brushed his lips against my forehead before trailing kisses down my cheek, each one more intoxicating than the last. It felt like a soft rain, gentle yet persistent, washing over me and leaving a trail of goosebumps in its wake.

By the time Archer moved closer, my heart was racing, and my skin tingled with anticipation. He captured my mouth in a deep, soul-stirring kiss. It felt like diving into deep waters, intense and overwhelming. The taste of him, the scent of his cologne, the feeling of his fingers tangled in my hair, it all combined to create a sensory overload.

I felt desired, cherished, and unbelievably aroused. The combination of their unique approaches, the varying pressures of their lips, the different textures of their touches, all fed into an ever-growing storm of need within me.

CHAPTER 28

VINNIE

I couldn't help the triumphant smirk tugging at the corner of my lips, seeing Becca's eyes clouded with desire. There was a silent agreement amongst the us, a shared understanding that in those moments, the only goal was to make Becca feel treasured.

We pulled her up from the bed and Isaac knelt, his eyes never leaving hers as he gently pulled down her sleep shorts and panties. The intent in his gaze had her biting her lip in anticipation. The four of us stood back for a moment, appreciating the sight of her. Soft, delicate, radiant. Every curve and angle of her body was a work of art.

My hands joined Luke's in lifting her shirt over her head, letting the fabric fall to the ground. Our fingers brushed against her skin, igniting a trail of fire. Archer, standing behind her, whispered praises into her ear, his deep voice making her shiver. Her perfect tits were exposed, and it was impossible to resist leaning in and bringing one of her nipples into my mouth, suckling on it until it hardened against my tongue.

With Becca bared to us, we each took a moment to

worship her. We feasted with our eyes first, taking in the flushed hue of her skin, the rapid rise and fall of her chest.

Taking a moment to breathe, I let my eyes rove over her body, and damn, what a sight to behold. The gentle dip of her waist, the luscious curve of her hips, and the soft swell of her breasts entranced me completely. The light in the room caught the hues of her hair, turning them into a shimmering cascade of golds and browns.

As I trailed my fingers over the curve of her side, I marveled at the softness and warmth under my touch.

Catching my stare, Becca smirked. "Enjoying the view, Vin?" Her voice dripped with playful challenge.

Grinning back, I leaned in, my lips hovering over hers. "Oh, darling, you have no idea. But let me show you just how much I'm into you."

Before I could make my move, however, Isaac was there first. "Actually," he said, a wolfish grin forming on his lips. "Let me start. I haven't had a chance to taste you yet."

Becca closed her eyes and bit her lower lip, her cheeks taking on a deeper tinge of red. "Who am I to deny the boss what he wants?"

Isaac smirked. "Good girl."

He swept her effortlessly off the ground, placing her on the edge of the bed and spreading her legs, revealing the pink, glistening line of her pussy. My cock stiffened even further at the sight of her bare before us. All I could think about was burying myself inside her, draining my seed deep. But first, it was Isaac's turn.

Isaac's skilled mouth went to work, his lips pressing soft, open-mouthed kisses on the inside of her thighs, teasing her until she was trembling with need. With a predatory grin, he slowly ran his tongue over her, and she gasped in aroused delight.

As Isaac worked, I took the opportunity to press soft kisses down her neck, my hands massaging her breasts. Archer and Luke knelt beside her, their fingers intertwined with hers as she opened their pants and took out their manhoods. She wrapped her slender fingers around their lengths, stroking them slowly as Isaac ate her out.

Each touch, each kiss, each whisper was orchestrated in a symphony of pleasure. As Isaac's pace increased, as he took her to dizzying heights, Becca's moans grew louder, more urgent.

When Becca's body finally tensed, her climax washing over her in waves, the satisfaction that filled me was indescribable. It wasn't my release, but seeing Becca come so hard was nearly as pleasurable as having an orgasm myself. She fell back onto the bed, her chest rising and falling as she recovered from the intensity.

Finally, with a sultry glint in her eye, Becca reached out for Isaac, beckoning him to her. The raw desire between them was palpable, sending a tingling sensation throughout the room.

"Come on," she said. "It's my turn to make *you* feel good."

With deliberate movements, she wrapped her legs around Isaac's hips, guiding him inside her. The moment they connected, a gasp bubbled from her lips.

From my vantage point, I could see the way Isaac's fingers gripped her waist, the muscles of his arms flexing with every thrust. Their rhythm was intoxicating - a dance of longing and satisfaction. The sight of her back arching, her breasts swaying with the intensity of his thrusts, had me aching with need. The room was filled with the music of their shared passion - every moan, every breathy whisper, pushing them closer to the pinnacle of pleasure.

Isaac's eyes never left hers, his gaze heavy with vigorous devotion. Every movement he made was calculated, aimed at maximizing her pleasure. And as the crescendo of their actions built, their shared climax was almost tangible, resonating throughout the room. He bucked into her over and over, the building of his pace hinting at how close he was to finishing. Finally, he erupted, letting out a hard grunt as he spilled inside.

When Isaac finished, he gently laid Becca down, their shared breaths heavy, eyes glazed with the aftermath of pleasure. Without missing a beat, Archer and Luke moved into position. Their intense, hungry stares only heightened the anticipation.

Becca positioned herself on all fours, giving the twins an inviting look. The sight of her in such a vulnerable yet empowering position, waiting to be claimed, was one I'll never forget. The play of light on her body highlighted every enticing curve, her skin glowing with a sheen of sweat and desire, her breasts swaying gently between her arms.

Archer took the lead, aligning himself behind her while Luke knelt in front, offering himself to her eager lips. Their synchronized movements, one of perfect understanding, showcased their shared history, a bond Becca now seamlessly fit into. Each thrust, each touch, was a testament to their unique connection.

The raw passion of the moment, the deep grunts and soft moans, filled the room. The vision of them together, Becca sandwiched between two powerful men, each dedicated to her pleasure, had my heart racing, my body thrumming with need. It was a dance of shadows and silhouettes, of gasps and sighs, and I was caught in its magnetic pull.

I had to catch my breath as Luke's climax mirrored Becca's, the sight one of intense pleasure. Luke's grip tightened on her hair, his face contorted in the throes of ecstasy. At the same moment, her body arched against Archer, a moan escaping her lips as he drove her to a shattering climax. Archer, losing himself in the rhythm of their shared passion, reached his peak moments later, collapsing beside her, both of them slick with sweat and satisfaction.

For a few minutes, the room was quiet save for the heavy breathing and low murmurs of satisfaction. Luke, Archer, and Isaac, each spent, reclined on the bed, the atmosphere thick with the haze of post-coital bliss. Their tangled limbs and sated expressions painted a picture of complete surrender.

I caught Becca's gaze from across the room, a teasing glint in her eye. "Looks like you're the last man standing, Vinnie," she purred, her voice dripping with playfulness and mischief.

I couldn't help but chuckle, feeling the weight of their collective gazes on us. "Seems so, doesn't it?" I replied with a smirk, my heart racing at the thought of our impending intimacy.

Motioning for her to come closer, I laid down and stretched out on the bed, propped up on my elbows. She crawled over, her body moving with a fluid, feline grace. She paused, hovering just above me, her hair cascading around her face like a silken curtain. Her lips were red from Luke's attention, her skin still flushed from her time with Archer.

"You ready for me?" she teased, her fingers tracing lazy patterns on my chest.

I reached up, gently pulling her down until her lips met mine in a slow, passionate kiss. "Always," I murmured against her mouth.

Guiding her, I positioned her above me. The sensation

of her sliding down onto me was one of pure ecstasy. The rest of the world melted away as she began to move, our bodies finding a rhythm that was uniquely ours.

There's something undeniably captivating about watching a woman lose herself in pleasure, especially from beneath her. From my vantage point, the view of Becca astride me was intoxicating. The sultry curves of her body, the rhythmic rise and fall of her hips, and the way the dim light of the room caressed her skin, highlighting every shadow and swell. I let my eyes wander over her, taking in the delicate arch of her neck as she threw her head back and the cascade of her hair brushing against my fingers.

Drawing her closer, I let my hands glide over her soft skin. They traveled from her hips, tracing the gentle curve of her waist, and finally, reaching her breasts. She moaned as I began to tease her nipples, rolling them between my fingers, feeling them harden under my touch. The sensation seemed to drive her wild, her movements becoming even more frenzied and eager. Her pussy felt perfect wrapped around me, warm and wet and tight.

Looking up into her eyes, I caught a flash of something profound. It was more than just lust—it was a connection, a deep-seated yearning. The kind that spoke of unspoken emotions and desires that transcended the physical. Our gazes locked, and for a split second, everything else ceased to exist. There was just her, me, and this powerful energy between us.

She began to ride me with a passion and intensity that took my breath away. Every movement, every shift, every arch of her back sent shockwaves of pleasure through my body.

"You feel so good," I managed to whisper, my voice

rough with desire. Her response was a soft moan, her rhythm increasing, driving us both closer to the edge.

As the pressure built, I gripped her hips, pulling her down harder onto me. She leaned forward, her forehead resting against mine, our breaths mingling as our pace became frantic. And then, as if on cue, the world shattered around us. Our bodies tensed, pleasure coursing through us in powerful, unrelenting waves. The force of our simultaneous climax left us breathless and spent, the aftershocks rippling through us.

Collapsing together, we took a moment to catch our breath, the weight of what had just transpired settling in. It was more than just a physical connection; it was an emotional one too.

We were a tangled mess of limbs and sheets, the five of us somehow fitting together on the bed as if it was made just for us. The afterglow was beautiful, a warm haze of satisfaction that blanketed the room, punctuated by occasional sighs and the soft caresses we lazily exchanged.

There I was, sandwiched between Becca and Isaac, her head resting on my shoulder while Isaac's fingers idly traced patterns on her back. The sense of comfort, of belonging, was overwhelming. It felt like we'd known each other forever, like we were pieces of a puzzle that had finally clicked into place.

Lost in my thoughts, I almost missed it when Isaac spoke.

"You know, I've never felt so... right." His voice was low, almost hesitant, but I knew exactly what he meant. The exact same sentiment had been running through my own mind moments before.

I looked at him, meeting his gaze, and nodded in agreement. There was no need for words. The emotion was clear in his eyes, and I'm sure he saw the same in mine.

Luke, lying on Becca's other side, leaned over and brushed a stray hair from her face. "Complicated doesn't even begin to describe it," he mused, voicing what we were all thinking.

Archer added, "But we've never been ones to shy away from a challenge, have we?"

Becca chuckled softly. "Guess not. But who would've thought the challenge would be this?"

The atmosphere in the room shifted, growing more serious. But instead of awkwardness, there was a sense of understanding, a silent pact forming between us. Even though we hadn't explicitly talked about the future and the complexities of the situation, it was clear: giving up wasn't an option. None of us were willing to let go of the magic we'd found together, no matter the obstacles.

"Honestly? I think we're all too stubborn to let anything stand in our way," Isaac commented.

The room erupted into soft laughter, lightening the mood. It was true. We were a determined bunch, always finding ways to overcome the hurdles life threw at us. And this unconventional relationship, as complicated as it was, felt worth every bit of effort.

Holding Becca close, I pressed a gentle kiss to her forehead. "Whatever comes our way," I whispered, "we'll handle it. Together."

She sighed contentedly, snuggling closer. "Together."

Lazily, we lay sprawled across the bed, the soft light filtering through the curtains casting a gentle glow on all of us. The scent of our earlier activities still lingered in the air, a testament to the passion we'd just shared. It was one of those perfect moments where everything seemed to pause, allowing us to bask in the comfort and warmth of each other's presence.

In that tranquil aftermath, nestled between the sheets, I found myself lost in thought. We all lay in a harmonious tangle, the ebb and flow of our breaths syncing up in a natural rhythm. As I felt Becca's soft exhale on my chest, my mind began painting images of our future.

I imagined Sunday breakfasts with laughter echoing, nights under a blanket of stars, shared responsibilities, and the joy of life's small moments – it all felt within reach. The very idea of us, in this unique bond, facing every tomorrow together, grew more and more enticing. That possibility of a harmonious, shared life, so different and yet so right, held an allure that tugged deeply at my heart.

It seemed perfect, like something I'd always yearned for but had never been able to imagine... until I met *her*.

However, our serenity was abruptly shattered when the door burst open. The five of us shot up at the same time, turning our attention to the figure standing at the entrance to the room.

Mikey stood in the hallway, eyes wide, staring at the scene before him. The color drained from his face, quickly replaced by a shade of furious red. "What the *fuck* is going on in here?" he roared, his voice echoing through the room.

Becca leapt from the bed, a sheet hastily wrapped around her, trying to form words to explain. "Mikey, calm down! It's not what you think!"

He didn't seem to hear her. Instead, his gaze was fixed on the four of us, anger and disbelief evident in his eyes. "Are you guys... did you hurt my sister?" His voice trembled with rage.

I was the first to act. Quickly pulling on my pants, I rose, my gaze locked on Mikey, ensuring he was the main focus. "Michael, I get that this is a shock. But believe me, no harm was done to Becca. Everything was consensual."

Vinnie, hands raised in a placating gesture, tried to approach him. "Hey, man, let's just talk, alright? It's not what it looks like. Just breathe and let's—"

But Mikey wasn't having it. He cut Vinnie off, his fury unmistakable. "You think this is a joke? This is my sister!" He stepped forward protectively, placing himself between Becca and us, every line of his body screaming defiance.

I could see Luke and Isaac, tense and ready to jump in if things turned physical, both hoping that wouldn't be the case. Slowly, we grabbed our clothes and dressed, Becca doing the same.

Becca, still trying to find her voice amid the chaos,

managed to pull Mikey slightly back. "Mikey, please listen to me. This... it's complicated, but you have to trust me. I'm okay. More than okay."

Mikey, visibly struggling to process everything, kept darting his gaze between Becca's pleading eyes and the four of us. His breath came in short bursts, and he seemed on the brink of either shouting again or possibly breaking down.

"Look, we can sit and talk about this," I began, trying to use my calmest tone. "No one wants to hide anything or lie. But bursting in like this and making accusations isn't going to help."

Mikey's jaw worked as he tried to find words, his emotions clearly warring inside him. We were on a precipice, the next few moments crucial in determining which way the situation would swing.

"They weren't hurting me. We're... together," Becca attempted to explain, her voice quivering slightly.

He blinked in disbelief, as if he couldn't comprehend what she was saying. His eyes flitted between us, narrowing suspiciously. "All of you?" he echoed, his voice rising. His words dripped with skepticism and a hint of disgust. "That's... no! There's no way! Becca..."

As my initial surprise waned, I took a closer look at Mikey. His movements seemed jittery, erratic. His eyes darted around with a glazed-over appearance, pupils dilated far beyond what the room's dimness justified. A cold realization dawned on me, sending a shiver down my spine. He didn't just seem surprised or outraged; something was off about his demeanor.

His speech, too, slurred slightly and his posture was all wrong. It hit me like a punch in the gut – Mikey might've been under the influence of something. The situation, already loaded with tension, suddenly felt even more precarious. The unexpected complexity of having him witness our intimacy while possibly being on some substance was a twist I hadn't seen coming.

Becca seemed to think the same thing, leaning forward to take a closer look at him. "Mikey, are you high right now?" she asked, an edge to her tone.

His face contorted, anger and shame fighting for dominance. "You're really lecturing me on being high when you're here with four dudes?" he spat, his voice laced with incredulity.

The fury behind his words set me on edge. All of us moved in unison, forming a protective barrier around Becca. It wasn't a conscious decision; it was instinctive. We were primed, ready to shield her from any harm.

"Back off," Becca commanded, her voice trembling but firm. "I can handle this."

Though we hesitated, our trust in Becca's judgment held us in place. We were a unit, and while we would have gladly thrown ourselves between Mikey and Becca, we also respected her wishes. But that didn't mean I was going to stand by idly. I was watching Mikey's every move, analyzing, ready to spring into action at the slightest hint of danger. A shocked brother was one thing – a drug user in the middle of a high was another.

His eyes darted between us, clearly agitated and disoriented. I could see the pain, the conflict waging within him. He was in over his head, and I could only hope Becca could reach him before things escalated further.

In those few, tense moments, I ran through countless scenarios in my head. My body was coiled like a spring, every muscle tensed, ready to intervene. If Mikey made a move, I had a plan. If things went south, I knew exactly how

I would get to Becca, how I'd position myself to ensure her safety.

The argument between Becca and Mikey exploded like a powder keg, their voices rising and filling the room with raw emotion.

"Why the hell are you doing this, Becca?" Mikey yelled, his voice dripping with accusation. "You're throwing yourself at them like... like some cheap--"

"Mikey!" Becca's voice cut through like a knife. "This isn't about them. This is about you and your damn addiction!"

The hurt was evident in both their voices. You could trace the history of pain and conflict between the siblings in each word exchanged.

A commotion from the doorway diverted my attention momentarily, and I saw Mary and Dad, both with expressions of bewilderment and concern. They had walked into the eye of a storm, and it was clear they were trying to process the volatile scene in front of them.

Mikey's anger momentarily redirected. "Oh, perfect! Now everyone can hear about how my sister's whoring herself out!"

Becca's face flushed red, her eyes flashing with hurt and anger. "You want to talk? Fine! How about your endless trips to rehab? The promises you've broken? The tears Mom's shed over you?"

The room seemed to close in on itself, each word slicing through the silence. Mary's face paled, absorbing the painful truths being laid bare, while Dad wore an expression of confusion and sorrow.

Mikey's face contorted with a mix of guilt and defiance. "So what? I have problems. But that doesn't make what you're doing okay!"

"And who are you to judge me?" Becca shot back, her voice quivering with emotion. "At least I'm not throwing my life away, chasing after the next high!"

As the heated words continued to flow, a myriad of emotions played out on Becca's face: anger, hurt, love, frustration. But underlying it all was a strength, a resilience I admired deeply. She was a fighter, battling not just for herself but for her family.

"You know what? Fuck this!" Mike's face contorted with anger as if he'd hit his limit.

In a split second, Mikey's anger took a physical turn. I saw the raw intent in his eyes as he raised his hand, poised to strike Becca. Without a second's hesitation, I lunged forward and gripped his raised wrist, stopping it in mid-air just inches from Becca's face.

Every fiber of my being screamed at me to teach Mikey a lesson he'd never forget. Who the fuck did he think he was? The thought of him even attempting to harm his own sister, especially when she was in such a vulnerable state, ignited a rage in me that was hard to contain. I could feel the fury rolling off Vinnie, Isaac, and Luke as well. We were a united front against any threat to Becca.

I tightened my grip on Mikey's wrist, looking directly into his eyes. "Calm down," I said, my voice firm and controlled. "This isn't the way."

Mikey, despite being caught in the grip of his anger, looked taken aback by the confrontation. His eyes darted between my face and his immobilized hand. "Screw you," he spat, his voice dripping with venom. "All of you can fuck off!"

I turned to Becca. She nodded, giving me the signal to release him. I let him go, my eyes never leaving him, silently challenging him to make another move. But instead, Mikey shot one last glare at us and stormed out, slamming the door behind him with enough force to rattle the windows.

Silence fell, save for the soft sounds of Becca and Mary crying. The weight of what had just transpired hung heavily in the room. Dad moved to comfort Mary, wrapping his arm around her shoulders as she buried her face in his chest. He then glanced at us, his eyes filled with disappointment and a hint of sadness.

"Finish getting dressed," Dad's voice was calm but authoritative. "We'll talk downstairs."

We all knew this was just the beginning of a difficult and potentially life-changing conversation. As I put on the rest of my clothes, my thoughts were a tumultuous whirlwind. Whatever the outcome, one thing was certain: things would never be the same.

The soft click of the door shutting felt like the final punctuation mark to the intense chapter of drama we'd all just witnessed. I was acutely aware of the four pairs of eyes on me, their gazes filled with concern and a hint of anxiety. The emotional weight of the confrontation with Mikey, the truths spilled, and the lingering tension had culminated into a pressure cooker moment, and I was struggling to keep it together.

Before I could even process what was happening, Luke stepped forward, reaching out to me. The gesture, so simple and full of genuine concern, was all it took. I crumpled into him, my body wracked with sobs. The dam of emotions I had tried to hold back burst forth, and tears streamed down my face.

I hated it. I felt so weak, so pathetic, like I couldn't handle anything. But as the guys held me, as I remained among their warmth, those sentiments faded.

The situation I was in the middle of would be hard as hell to navigate. However, I didn't have to do it alone.

Luke held me tightly, his strong arms encircling me, and

I took solace in his warmth. I felt hands on my back, fingers gently brushing my hair, a comforting presence right behind me. The realization that all of them, Archer, Vinnie, Isaac, and Luke, were rallying around me, providing a shield against the storm of emotions, made me feel anchored amidst the chaos.

"Hey, hey," Archer murmured softly, his voice filled with that cool, composed tone I had come to rely on. "We've got you. It's going to be okay."

Vinnie chimed in, his voice warm and comforting, "We're not going anywhere, alright? We're right here with you."

I sniffled, pulling away from Luke slightly to look at them, my eyes red and puffy. "I'm so sorry you guys had to see that," I whispered, feeling a fresh wave of guilt for exposing them to my family's dysfunctions.

Isaac gently brushed a stray tear from my cheek. "It's okay, Becca," he reassured me. "Families are messy. It's how you handle the mess that matters."

"They're right," Luke added, pressing a soft kiss to my forehead. "We're in this together, for better or worse."

Hearing those words, feeling their unwavering support, I took a deep breath. Despite the tumultuous events of the day, I found strength in the knowledge that I wasn't alone. I had them.

But as the reality of the situation began to sink in, a knot of anxiety formed in my stomach. Things had changed, the dynamics shifted. This was going to be tough.

"I don't think I'm ready for this conversation," I admitted.

The guys nodded.

"We're ready," Isaac said. "And don't forget we're here for you."

There was nothing to do but go through it. We left the room together, making our way downstairs.

The warm, rich colors of the living room seemed to intensify as I stepped in, Mom's familiar space looking different in the wake of everything that had happened. I made my way to her, our shared pain pulling us together, and we clung to each other, our mutual tears mingling.

After a moment that felt suspended in time, my mother took a step back, her face showing the combination of love, concern, and confusion that was so quintessentially her. Sal was there, still and calm, his presence reassuring despite the fact that he was no doubt wrestling with what he'd just learned.

Mikey's absence was like a black void in the room. Though our confrontation had been harsh, I couldn't shake off the concern for him. His recent actions, the drugs, the anger, they weren't him. Not really. Not the Mikey I grew up with. The weight of worry pressed on my heart.

"Becca," she started, her voice firmer than before, "I need you to sit down and tell me everything. Let's start with your brother."

I nodded, moving to the couch. The four of them - Archer, Luke, Isaac, and Vinnie - seemed to move in silent agreement. Archer and Vinnie sat on either side of me, while Isaac and Luke stood behind the couch, almost like sentinels. I could feel the weight of their nearness, their unspoken support.

I glanced at my mother and saw her exchanging a significant look with Sal filled with understanding, questions, and decisions. Taking a deep breath, my words came out slowly, filled with hesitation but also determination.

"Mom, I know how everything looks. And I can't even begin to express how sorry I am that all of this is coming out this way. Especially about Mikey." I paused, sucked in a breath, and continued. "He's been struggling. It's been really hard for both of us since Dad left. He found solace in the wrong places, and it just... spiraled from there. He's been in and out of rehabs, and every time I think he's getting better, he relapses."

Mom appeared shocked. "You're telling me he's still using? I thought this was all behind him. Just college stuff he'd grown out of."

"That's what I thought, too. I didn't find out he was still using until a few years ago. And... God, I wanted to tell you, knew I should've told you. But every time he managed to convince me to keep it a secret. I guess I figured that if he could put this all behind him then you'd never have to worry."

Mom said nothing, tears shimmering in her eyes. I felt like scum, like a total liar. But if Mom was mad about Mikey, she didn't say it. Sal handed her a nearby box of tissues, and she quickly wiped her eyes.

"And you and the boys. What is this?"

I paused for a moment, gathering my thoughts, knowing the next part of the conversation would be even trickier.

"As for the four of them," I gestured toward Archer, Luke, Isaac, and Vinnie, "it's not what you think. Then again, I don't know what you think. It's a very unusual situation. I know how unconventional and confusing it might sound. And honestly, if you'd told me a few months ago this would be my life, I wouldn't have believed it." I laughed quietly, self-deprecatingly. "But somehow, in the midst of the craziness of life, they've become a part of mine. Each of them, in their own unique way, brings something into my life. It's not about lust or rebellion. It's more profound than that. It's about love, understanding, and support. And before you say anything, I want you to know they've treated me with nothing but respect."

I took another shaky breath, my eyes filling with tears. "I know this isn't easy for you to hear. And believe me, Mom, I wish there was an easier way to explain everything. But I need you to understand that this is my life. These choices, as unconventional as they are, have been made with a lot of thought. I just... I hope, in time, you can come to accept them. And maybe even understand."

There, it was all out. Every uncomfortable truth laid bare. Now it was up to my mom and Sal to process it.

Once I'd finished, a heavy silence draped over us. I could feel the intense emotions filling the room, everyone lost in their thoughts. My heart raced, waiting for a response, for judgment, for something.

Mom broke the silence. "Thank you for being honest," she said softly. But her eyes held a storm of emotions that told me this conversation was far from over. Her face paled slightly, her gaze searching mine for more answers. "Tell me more about your brother." The worry was plainly evident in her voice.

"Okay, Mom," I responded, trying to steady my own voice, but the weight of it all, combined with the recent confrontation, made it challenging. "He's been... it's been bad. Ever since he got involved with the wrong crowd and the drugs, he's been spiraling. Like I said, every time I thought he was finally getting better, he'd relapse. The rehabs... they're expensive, but I thought they were his best shot. So, I've been trying to help him, paying for the facilities as best as I could."

Mom's hand flew to her mouth, her eyes moistening. "Why didn't you tell me?"

"I didn't want to worry you," I confessed, blinking back

tears. "You've been through so much, and with you finding happiness with Sal, I didn't want to burden you further."

The silence in the room was deafening. Archer's and Luke's comforting hands were a gentle weight on my legs, grounding me amidst the turbulence of emotions.

"Becca," Isaac's voice broke the silence, "you didn't have to shoulder all of this alone. We would have helped if you'd told us."

I looked up at him, my throat tightening, and managed a small, grateful smile. "Thank you, Isaac. It's just hard to ask for help with something so personal, you know?"

Mom took a moment to process everything, exhaling slowly. "Beck, I wish you'd told me. We could have faced it together. And these guys," she said, gesturing to the four of them, "clearly they care about you."

I nodded. "I know, Mom. It was just hard for me to accept that this was happening to him. That my little brother, who I'd always tried to protect, was falling apart, and there was so little I could do."

Sal, who had been silent until now, finally spoke. "We'll find a way to help him, together. But he also needs to want to help himself. I've dealt with addicts before. You can only do so much for them unless they *want* to get better."

"I know. I just hope it's not too late."

Mom wrapped her arms around me, holding me tight, and for a brief moment, I felt safe despite all the craziness in my life.

Mom's eyes welled with tears, her hand resting on my cheek. "What's been going on with my son?" she asked out loud to no one in particular. "My baby boy."

"Mikey was so ashamed, Mom. He thought he could handle it, and I wanted to believe him. I threatened to tell you if he got high while we were here. I just... I thought if he had some sense of responsibility, of someone waiting for him to get better, he would try harder."

Pulling back, I looked at her, tears streaming down my face. "I'm so sorry, Mom. I thought he'd get better. But it's so much worse than I could've imagined."

Mom's eyes searched mine. "How bad, Beck?"

I took a deep breath, searching for the right words, "Real bad. There were times I'd get calls in the middle of the night, not knowing where he was or what he had taken. Times I'd find him passed out, barely breathing. It's scary bad."

A chilling silence enveloped the room. The air felt heavy, the undercurrent of tension almost palpable. We all sensed it - a feeling of foreboding. Mikey's situation wasn't just a problem anymore; it was a looming crisis.

Sal leaned forward, his expression serious. "We'll help him. But first, we need to find him."

Mary nodded slowly, though her eyes spoke of the pain she felt. "I just wish I had known. I wish I could've been there for him."

I felt a hand squeeze mine and turned to see Archer, his eyes filled with understanding. "We're here now, Becca. All of us. And we'll all face whatever comes next. You're not alone in this anymore."

Sal's imposing presence brought a weighty silence in the room, and all eyes turned to him. His gaze was steady, exuding an authority hard to ignore.

"We've addressed one issue, but we have another elephant in the room that needs further discussion," Sal began, nodding subtly toward Becca and the rest of us.

The implication was clear. We'd brushed over the matter, but now there was no option but to discuss what was happening.

I held back, preferring to gauge the situation. While I wasn't blood, Sal had always made me feel like part of the family, and I had a fierce loyalty to him. However, this was a delicate matter, and I wasn't about to dive in headfirst without knowing the depth of the water.

Before I could piece together my thoughts, Archer spoke up. "Dad, I know this might not be easy for you and Mary to hear, but what Becca and we have... it's real. It might be unconventional, but it's genuine."

Vinnie chimed in. "We never meant for it to be a secret.

It just... happened. And we didn't want to spring it on everyone, especially with the wedding news."

Sal raised a hand, asking for silence. The room hushed immediately. "I've always taught you boys to lead with your hearts, to be honest, and to be true to yourselves." He paused, letting his words sink in. "But Becca is our family now. Or is about to be. This complicates things."

Becca looked a little defensive. "I never expected any of this. The care and bond I share with them... it's real, Mr. Gallo. I promise."

"Sal, please," he said, offering a brief but warm smile.

I felt the need to contribute. "We understand the concerns, and believe me, we've discussed them at length. We want to make sure Becca is always treated with respect and love."

Sal sighed heavily, rubbing his temples. "This isn't easy for any of us. But I trust my boys, and I trust Becca. If this is what all of you want, then I'll support it." His gaze shifted to Mary, who nodded slowly in agreement.

The room seemed to let out a collective breath, the tension ebbing away. This wasn't the end of the discussion by any means, but for now, there was a semblance of understanding, a bridge to potentially navigate these choppy waters.

I watched as Archer leaned forward, his confidence sure even in this heavy atmosphere. "When this all started, none of us expected it to become more than just some fun. We didn't plan this." Archer looked between Sal and Mary, sincerity etching his features. "But somewhere over time, things changed. Profoundly. It isn't just about fun anymore."

Sal's eyes narrowed, a mix of surprise and caution. He had always been protective, and watching his expression change was like witnessing a storm brew, unsure of where the lightning would strike.

"I've fallen for Becca," Archer's voice was steady, unwavering. "And I'm not going to hide it. I'm not ashamed of it."

Mary's gaze shot to Becca, her maternal instincts clear as day. "And you, Becca? How do you feel about all this?"

Becca took a deep breath, her cheeks flushing. "I know how it sounds. I know it's crazy, even to me." She met Mary's gaze, her voice raw with emotion. "But it's the truth. I've fallen for them too. All of them."

A weighted silence fell over the room. You could've heard a pin drop. Everyone seemed to be processing, trying to make sense of the emotions swirling around.

Sal took a moment, then slowly rose from his seat. He approached Becca, placing a gentle hand on her shoulder. "Life has a way of surprising us, throwing things at us that we never see coming." He looked at each of his sons in turn, then back at Becca. "But at the end of the day, if you all truly care for one another, who am I to stand in the way?"

This was a surprising twist. Coming from Sal, who was otherwise a pretty traditional guy, it felt surreal. I knew, though, that beneath his rough exterior was a heart that genuinely wished the best for his family.

Mary added, "I just want my daughter to be happy. Safe. Loved."

I could tell she was struggling with the situation, as any mother would. But Becca wasn't a child, and Mary seemed to recognize that.

Becca blinked back tears, pulling Mary into a hug. "I am loved, Mom. More than I ever thought possible."

The night had taken us on an emotional rollercoaster, but for now, the car seemed to be pulling back into the station. We were all processing, trying to understand this tangled web we'd found ourselves in.

Vinnie cleared his throat, drawing all eyes to him. His usual jovial demeanor was tempered with seriousness. "I'm in love with Becca too," he confessed, looking at Sal with an earnestness that surprised me. Vinnie was rarely this vulnerable, and it drove home just how significant this situation was to all of us.

Luke stood up, pushing himself off the couch. "Dad, I know this is... uncharted territory for our family. It will make all of us truly happy, though."

Sal's gaze, heavy with contemplation, finally shifted to me. I felt the weight of his expectations, the history between us as the unofficial fourth son.

Taking a deep breath, I began, "Sal, you've always treated me like one of your own. And for that, I'm eternally grateful." I paused, picking my words carefully. "We understand the implications of this relationship, especially now. None of us wants to bring shame or disrespect to you, Mary, or ourselves. We love each other, genuinely. And we believe we can build something meaningful with Becca."

I took another breath, trying to steady my emotions. "Our hope, our collective wish, is that this doesn't harm any of the relationships we cherish. Whether it's our bond with you, Becca's with her mom, or even your relationship with Mary. We want to be a united family."

A few beats of silence filled the room, each one of us holding our breath, waiting for Sal's response.

He sighed heavily, and I could see the weight of our revelations pressing on him. He looked around at each of us, his gaze thoughtful. "If there's one thing I've learned over the years, it's that love can't be dictated by society's norms or expectations. It's a force all its own."

Sal met Mary's eyes, who smiled gently at him, then looked at Becca. "However, whatever path you all choose, be sure it's one you're ready for. Not just in the joyous times, but also when the storm clouds gather. Love is a commitment, a responsibility."

Luke nodded. "We know, Dad. We're ready."

Sal took a deep breath, nodding in return. "Then all I can offer is my support. It might take some time to adjust, for all of us. But as long as you're respectful and treat each other right, I'll be in your corner."

A silent communication passed between Sal and Mary, the sort of unspoken conversation only those deeply connected could hold. It wasn't unlike the way the rest of us connected with each other or Becca.

Mary stepped forward, her gaze softening as it met Becca's. She cupped her daughter's face tenderly. "Darling, remember that no matter what, I love you. That will never change."

Sal echoed her sentiments, looking at each of us in turn. "You're all my family, blood or not. That won't change either."

Before they could make their exit, worry creased Mary's features. "I just can't shake the feeling that Mikey is spiraling out there. With everything that's happened... I'm afraid of where his head might be."

Determination flashed across Becca's face. "I'll find him, Mom," she promised.

I felt a twinge of concern. I didn't like the idea of Becca potentially putting herself in harm's way, even if it was for her brother. I bit my tongue, knowing now wasn't the moment to voice my reservations.

Mary nodded, squeezing Becca's hand before turning to

leave with Sal. The weight of their departure settled on the room, leaving us all in contemplative silence.

Then, breaking the quiet, Becca announced firmly, "We're getting Mikey out of whatever mess he's gotten himself into."

Vinnie was the first to speak, his tone gentle yet filled with concern, "Are you sure that's wise? It could be nothing – might've just gone for a walk to clear his head."

"Maybe. But if he's in danger, I have to do something," Becca retorted, her voice laced with both frustration and worry. "He's my brother."

Luke chimed in, "We're all in this together. Whatever we decide, we do it as a team."

Archer nodded in agreement. "Mikey needs help. And we need a plan."

I watched Becca closely, admiring her resolve. Her bond with Mikey was clear, and her willingness to step into the fray to help him was both admirable and frightening. I knew in that moment, whatever the plan, I'd stand by her side, ready to face whatever came our way. The sentiment was silently shared among all of us; we were a team, and nothing was going to stand in our way.

CHAPTER 32

LUKE

The room buzzed with tension and anticipation as we all considered how to tackle the Mikey situation. It'd already been a few hours since he left, and that was more than enough time for an addict to get up to trouble. Watching Becca worry about him made it impossible to stand idly by.

Sal squared his shoulders. "Mary and I will take a few areas and start the search."

"No, wait," Becca intervened, catching them before they could get up. She wore a look that conveyed she wanted to protect her mother from any more distress, if only for a while. "Let me handle Mikey. Give yourselves some time to think, process everything, like you said. I promise we'll take care of it."

Sal looked ready to protest, but a soft touch on his arm from Mary halted him. He nodded silently. "She's right," he murmured, his eyes meeting Becca's. "We need some time. And it's a good idea for us to hold down the fort here in case he comes back. Let's go upstairs, okay?"

Mary nodded in a manner that made it clear she was

still in something of a daze from the conversation we'd just had. Dad staying here with her was the right call.

Sal's gaze rested on each of us, finally landing on me. I nodded reassuringly. As they headed upstairs, I could feel the weight of responsibility on our collective shoulders, the unspoken promise that we would bring Mikey home safely.

The bedroom door upstairs had barely closed behind them when Becca's tone shifted from concerned sister to resourceful woman on a mission. "No need to split up or search blindly. I've had an Airtag on Mikey's phone for a while now." She gave a sheepish smile. "Big sister instincts. I've always worried he'd get lost one day, quite literally."

I grinned despite the situation. "Always one step ahead, aren't you?"

Isaac raised an eyebrow, clearly impressed. "That's smart."

She shrugged, opening her laptop. "I wanted to be prepared. Now, let's see where my wayward brother has taken himself."

We all huddled around as she brought up a tracking app. A blip on the screen indicated Mikey's location.

Vinnie let out a whistle. "Well, he's not that far. Looks to be about three miles from here."

Archer looked thoughtful, his strategic mind plotting. "We should approach cautiously. We don't know the kind of people he's with or what state he's in."

Becca's fingers danced over the keyboard, pulling up a street view of the location. A rundown building, graffiti-covered, and looking all sorts of suspicious, greeted our eyes.

"That's our spot," Becca declared, determination in her voice.

I felt a surge of protectiveness, not just for Becca, but for Mikey as well. "Alright," I said, taking charge, "We'll go there, scope out the scene. If anything goes sideways, I want us to all be there together."

Becca nodded in agreement. This was family, and when family was on the line, we took no chances. We were going in prepared, and we would bring Mikey home. Safe. We headed out, taking our rental car.

The SUV's engine purred beneath us, the smooth rumble cutting through the silence that had settled within the vehicle. In the confines of the car, the atmosphere was dense. The combination of concern for Mikey and the unresolved questions about the nature of our relationship with Becca weighed down the mood. As the afternoon air rushed by, the shadows from the trees outside played a silent dance on the road.

I let out a slow breath, trying to keep my composure, then turned my attention to Becca. In the low light, I could see her profile, lips slightly parted, eyes fixed ahead, lost in thought. I reached over, taking her hand, feeling the warmth of her fingers intertwined with mine. "You doing okay?"

She blinked and looked at me, surprise evident in her eyes as if she'd forgotten for a moment that she wasn't alone in her worries. "Yeah," she began slowly, "I mean, considering the circumstances, I'm holding up. Just worried about my brother."

I squeezed her hand, attempting to convey as much comfort as I could. "We'll find him. And we'll help him. That's a promise."

My thoughts began to drift back to the challenges ahead. Becca seemed to sense the shift in my mood, her fingers squeezing mine. "Hey," she whispered, her voice soft, "we'll get through this, alright? All of it."

I nodded, pulling her close. "Together."

She snuggled against my side, and I kissed the top of her head.

"I was just thinking about something," she started, the edges of her lips curling upward.

I watched her closely, curious. "What's on your mind?"

Becca's gaze fixed on the winding road ahead, her eyes glazed in remembrance. "I was thinking about this one summer, when Mikey and me were kids playing near the woods behind our old house."

I said nothing, taking her hand and letting her reminisce. She smiled, squeezing my hand back.

She chuckled softly. "I was trying to climb a tree, wanting to build a treehouse or something silly like that. But I was a little too ambitious and chose the tallest tree I could find. I managed to get pretty high up, but then got scared and couldn't come back down. I was about ten years old. I got stuck up there for an hour. Then, sure enough, Mikey showed up."

She nodded, smiling at the memory. "He was so mad at me for climbing so high. But instead of scolding me, he scaled that tree like it was nothing. He came up, calmed me down, and then helped me climb down, step by step." She paused, her voice softer. "He always looked out for me, you know? Whenever I did something reckless, he was always there to help, even though he was the younger one."

I could imagine a young Mikey, all gangly limbs, his face set in determination, doing whatever it took to make sure his sister was safe. The bond between them was evident.

She sighed deeply, the smile fading a little. "He saved me and now I'm trying to save him."

The weight of the situation settled back on us, and I looked at the matter from her point of view. Mikey, once the reliable brother, had lost his way. And it was now up to Becca to help guide him back.

I pulled her close, my arm wrapping around her shoulders. "He's lucky to have you, Becca. And so are we."

"Thanks." Her voice wavered, the emotions from the past mingling with the weight of the present. The corners of her eyes glistened with unshed tears. I could feel the subtle tremor in her hand as it gripped my arm, and it was evident how the magnitude of everything was getting to her.

Vinnie leaned forward and placed a gentle hand on her knee. "Hey," he began softly, "you don't always have to be the strong one, you know?"

Becca's eyes met his, the strength in her gaze slightly overshadowed by the shimmering tears.

"That strength of yours, it's one of the things we all adore about you," Isaac chimed in, his voice filled with warmth. "But remember, you're not alone in this. We're here, and we'll help carry the weight."

She blinked, the tears spilling over and tracing lines down her cheeks. Without a word, she shifted closer and buried her face in my shoulder. Her body trembled with restrained sobs. I wrapped my arms around her, pulling her close, feeling the warmth of her body against mine. Archer reached over, gently rubbing her back, while Vinnie took one of her hands in his, squeezing it reassuringly.

She looked up at me, her eyes glistening. "We just have to find him, Luke. Before it's too late."

I nodded, pressing a kiss to her forehead. "We will. We have each other. And together, we're unstoppable."

Becca drew in a deep breath, and I could sense a shift in her. The vulnerability was still there, but layered over it was her signature determination. We drove in silence for a few moments, our shared concern for Mikey closing in on all of us.

The neighborhood we approached gradually transformed. Gone were the manicured lawns and quaint houses. They were replaced by cracked pavements, graffiti-sprayed walls, and houses that had seen far better days. The buildings had a worn-out, defeated look to them, some with boarded-up windows and unkempt yards littered with discarded items.

The scant number of people we saw moved with a shuffle, their eyes scanning the surroundings, wary of any potential threat. An old car, rust eating its edges, rumbled past us, its engine sputtering more than purring.

We finally pulled up in front of a particularly dilapidated house. Its paint was peeling, the porch sagged, and I noticed a couple of windows on the upper floor were shattered. There was an air of abandonment, though a dim light shone through a gap in the thick curtains of one of the windows. Sounds of a muffled argument leaked through the walls, punctuated by a laugh with more madness in it than mirth.

Archer leaned forward from the backseat, his gaze sharp. "Are you sure this is the place?"

Becca glanced at her phone again, double-checking the Airtag's location. "Yeah, this is it."

Isaac's eyes were hard, his protective instincts evident. "We should go in together. Stay close, and don't engage unless necessary."

I caught her hand and squeezed. "You ready for this?"

She paused, her eyes searching the house once more. The trepidation was clear in her gaze, but she set her jaw and nodded. "As ready as I'll ever be."

CHAPTER 33

BECCA

Stepping onto the creaky porch of the dilapidated house, a chill ran down my spine. The feeling was oppressive, as if dark things happened within these walls. Every possible negative outcome ran through my head, and I had to push back a horrifying image of finding him lifeless inside, arriving just a little too late to prevent the overdose that finally did him in.

But as much as fear threatened to consume me, the presence of the guys surrounding me was like a protective shield. Luke was at my left, his eyes never leaving mine, communicating silent reassurances. To my right, Vinnie was scanning the surroundings, while Archer was right behind me, and Isaac was a few steps ahead, taking point.

Mustering all the courage I had, I raised my fist and knocked, the sound echoing ominously. The door was opened a crack by a gaunt man, his eyes bloodshot and his face lined with the evidence of years of hard living. He eyed us suspiciously, especially noting the four men who towered around me.

"Who're you?" he rasped, voice dripping with suspicion.

"I'm here for Mikey," I said as calmly as I could manage, trying not to let the desperation show in my voice. "Is he here?"

The man's eyes darted back and forth between me and the guys. He seemed to be weighing his options. "Don't know no Mikey," he lied, his voice taking on a defiant tone.

I tried a softer approach, desperation sneaking into my tone. "Please, he's my brother. I just want to make sure he's okay."

Before he responded, the door was suddenly slammed in our faces, the sound of multiple locks being thrown into place echoing through the silence. A wave of panic hit me, my mind racing as I tried to figure out our next move.

However, before I could react, Isaac took a step forward, bracing his shoulder against the door, and with a display of raw strength, shoved until the door came completely off its hinges. It crashed to the floor with a deafening thud, leaving the druggie stunned, gaping at the doorway now void of any barrier.

Breathing heavily, I turned to Isaac with a hint of awe. "Well, that's one way to do it," I commented with a shaky laugh.

Isaac winked at me, his stance strong and unwavering, "Always here to open doors for you."

The man backed away, holding his hands up, clearly out of his depth. "Look, I don't want no trouble," he stammered.

Neither did I, but we were already knee-deep in it. We just had to wade through and find Mikey.

Walking into the house was like stepping into a grim alternate universe. The stench hit me first — a nauseating mix of body odor, stale cigarette smoke, and something acrid that I couldn't quite place but which instantly set my nose wrinkling. The walls, possibly once white, were now a dingy yellow with splotches of brown and other unidentifiable stains. They seemed to absorb the meager light coming through the grime-caked windows, making the entire place seem eternally dim.

The floorboards beneath my feet groaned with every step, and I couldn't help but feel they might give way under our collective weight. The living room we'd entered looked like a snapshot of misery. Tattered, moth-eaten couches, their stuffing erupting from various tears, littered the spaces, surrounded by all manner of debris: empty food containers, discarded needles, and overturned beer cans. Dirty mattresses lay here and there, bearing their own disturbing marks of wear and tear.

In one corner, a junkie was slumped over, so still my heart seized in fear. But then I noticed the faint rise and fall of his chest, his life still clinging on in this hellish place. Another woman, skeletal thin with hair like matted straw, was scratching absently at her arm, her vacant eyes never leaving the floor.

The junkie who'd locked the door was now against the wall, his eyes darting around the room in panic. He looked like a cornered rat, his hollow cheeks twitching and sweat forming on his brow. Every muscle in his scrawny frame seemed to vibrate with tension, clearly convinced he was about to get a thorough beating from the four guys.

Archer, his demeanor calm and even, took a step forward. "We're not here to hurt you," he said, though his voice had an edge that conveyed he meant business. "We just want Mikey. Where is he?"

The junkie's Adam's apple bobbed as he swallowed hard. "Young guy, right? Wiry, with blue eyes? He's... he's in the back," he stammered, his gaze darting toward a hallway leading deeper into the house. "But you need to take him and get the fuck out – fast."

"What's the hurry?" Vinnie inquired, narrowing his eyes.

The junkie's voice dropped to a barely audible whisper, fear evident in every syllable. "The Garcias. They run this place. If they catch you here, especially with Mikey..." he trailed off, leaving the implications hanging in the heavy air.

The blood drained out of my face. "We need to find him. Now." I had no idea who the Garcias were, but something told me I didn't want to be here if they showed up.

I moved toward the hallway. The guys quickly took up positions, Vinnie and Isaac guarding the entrance while Archer and Luke kept watch from the living room, ensuring I had a clear path to and from the back of the house. I stepped over the threshold of the bedroom, gasping at what I saw.

Mikey's form was hard to distinguish among the squalor. The room seemed even smaller than the others, the air thick with the foul stench of decay and stale smoke. Worn-out wallpaper peeled from the walls in lifeless strips, and a broken window was patched up with cardboard and plastic. The acrid smell of meth and other substances I couldn't identify cloaked the room– a choking aroma that made my eyes water and my throat burn.

The feeble light from the hallway revealed Mikey sprawled out on a filthy mattress. His skin was a pale, clammy shade, contrasting starkly with the dark circles under his eyes. His breaths came in shallow, uneven rasps, his chest barely moving. As I approached, I noticed his lips had taken on a bluish tint. It felt like a cold hand grasped my heart.

"Mikey," I whispered, my voice trembling as I reached

out to shake him gently. His eyelids fluttered momentarily but didn't open, and he a low, throaty moan tumbled out of his mouth. Panic bubbled up inside me. What had he taken? Was he dying?

I took a deep breath, trying to keep my rising panic at bay. "Mikey, it's Becks," I coaxed, touching his face and feeling the clammy coldness of his skin. I wished fervently for some sign of recognition, a flicker in his eyes, a twitch of his mouth – anything.

Footsteps echoed behind me. I turned to see Isaac entering the room, his face etched with concern. Without a word, he bent down beside me, checking Mikey's pulse and then gently slapping his cheeks, trying to rouse him.

"He needs a doctor," Isaac said, his voice filled with urgency.

Behind him, Archer and Vinnie entered. Vinnie knelt, taking in Mikey's state, while Archer looked around the room, his eyes scanning for any immediate dangers.

"We need to get him out of here, fast," Vinnie said. He and Isaac carefully hoisted Mikey up, supporting him between them as they made their way back to the living room.

As I trailed behind the guys, my heart thudded painfully against my chest, each beat echoing the weight of the fear and desperation clawing at me. Mikey's usually animated face was hauntingly pallid, his eyelids fluttering weakly. Every shallow breath he took sent an icy lance of terror through my spine. The ominous shadows cast by the dilapidated buildings around us seemed to mock our frantic escape, whispering of the impending doom we might be facing.

"Mikey, please," I murmured as I watched Isaac and Luke support the bulk of his weight. My fingers clung to the cold skin of his wrist, desperate to feel the reassuring thud of his pulse. Memories of our childhood rushed back — Mikey chasing after me in the garden, shielding me from neighborhood bullies, always being the doting little brother. The idea of a world without him was unimaginable.

His lips, tinged with a dangerous shade of blue, quivered, and he managed a weak groan, forcing his eyelids open just a fraction. My heart soared.

"Becca," he rasped, the word barely more than a breath. But it was the most beautiful sound I'd ever heard. He was still in there, still fighting, and I would move heaven and earth to keep it that way.

As we moved toward the exit, a rush of adrenaline propelled me forward, pushing away the nausea and dread threatening to overwhelm me. My only focus was on getting my brother to safety, hoping it wasn't too late.

As we stepped into the cool winter air, the relative silence was broken by the menacing rumble of engines. Before we could fully process the situation, a small fleet of cars barreled down the street, skidding to a halt, creating a makeshift barricade in front of the dilapidated house. Dust swirled, and from the shadows of the vehicles, figures emerged.

Each of them looked rougher than the last — leather jackets, tattoos snaking down arms, chains hanging from pockets. But it was their eyes that truly terrified me. Cold, calculating, and hungry, they sized us up like prey.

The silence was thick, almost suffocating, broken only when one of them stepped forward. "Where you think you're going with him?" he drawled, his voice dripping with menace. His gaze was fixed on Mikey, who was still groggy but beginning to show signs of awareness.

I swallowed hard, readying myself to answer when Vinnie replied. "Taking our friend home."

The man sneered, revealing a gold tooth. "He owes me a hell of a lot of money. And you think you can just waltz out with him?" He stepped forward slowly, fury in his eyes. "Not a goddamn chance."

CHAPTER 34

ISAAC

Surrounded by the harsh cacophony of growling engines and sharp, muttered exchanges, my focus narrowed on our immediate surroundings. We were in a damn tight spot.

The pulsing beat of adrenaline surged through my veins, and though my instinct screamed to draw the line and defend, I knew the best option was to remain poised. Cool heads would need to prevail here.

I could sense the energy of the group of men who must be the Garcias, a collective menace that seemed to emanate from their ranks, and it was nothing to be trifled with. It was clear we were on their turf, and while we had the immediate objective of getting Mikey out safely, there was a larger game afoot. Respect, territory, and a display of power. Those were always the undercurrents in situations like this.

Becca's voice, rising in defiant determination, pulled me back to the moment. "We're taking my brother and we're leaving," she declared, chin lifted. It was a bold move, but it was also Becca—she wouldn't stand down when family was on the line.

In stark contrast to her statement, the Garcia's leader, a

mountain of a man with scars that hinted at a past of violence, responded. The slow, predatory grin he wore heightened the anxiety coursing through me.

"He isn't going anywhere without settling his dues," he rumbled, voice laden with a thinly veiled threat.

My heart raced, and not for the first time, I felt the weight of the choices we had made. The situation was teetering dangerously close to a point of no return. Behind me, I sensed Archer tensing up, ready to spring into action, while Luke subtly moved, positioning himself between the gang and Becca. Vinnie's eyes darted around, calculating exits and formulating strategies.

But it was clear, even to the Garcias, that any overt move on our part would light the fuse to an explosive standoff.

I locked eyes with the leader. The silent understanding was evident—we both knew the score. Power, respect, and the unspoken rules of the street were at play. Mikey's debt was just the face of it. The deeper issue? This was a challenge. A test of resolve.

Every muscle in my body was coiled tight. The silence stretched, pregnant with tension, making every second feel like an eternity. The Garcias, clearly confident in their numbers and firepower, waited for our move. And as the standoff persisted, the gnawing dread in my gut intensified. All it would take was a single misstep, one wrong word, and the situation could erupt into violence.

Becca, her face a fierce mix of concern and defiance, stepped forward with a bite to her tone. "We're not paying you a cent," she declared, the words slicing through the tension like a blade, "and consider yourselves lucky we're not dialing 911 right now."

Shit. I winced at her playing that card. Mentioning the

police in a situation like this was akin to tossing a match into a pile of dry leaves. It would only make things worse.

I leaned toward her, my voice low but firm. "Becca, this isn't the time for bluffs. Let's keep it cool, okay?" My hand gently pressed on her arm, attempting to ground her, to pull her back from the precipice of emotion she teetered upon.

She hesitated, her eyes scanning mine, searching for any hint of a plan or guidance. I could see the moment she decided to hand me the reins, her chin dipping in a subtle nod.

With a deep breath, I squared my shoulders, addressing the looming figure of the Garcia leader. "How much does he owe?" My voice was even, stripped of any challenge, but it carried an undercurrent of steely determination.

The leader eyed me, his face unreadable, before finally revealing the amount. "Five grand. " The tone was mocking yet tinged with genuine confusion. Why would someone willingly put themselves in such debt? Had Mikey planned on getting enough drugs for one last binge, one that would end his life?

I pushed the thought out of my head, turning my attention to Archer. I nodded to him, and he nodded right back.

Without missing a beat, Archer reached into his pocket, fingers expertly fishing out a thick wad of cash, his hand going up as he did to assure the Garcias he wasn't trying anything funny. As a precaution, we'd stopped at a bank before coming to this hellhole. Archer had pulled out several thousand dollars, just in case. Our motto is like the Boy scouts: always be prepared.

I took the cash, fanning it out slightly for emphasis. "Ten thousand," I declared, holding the leader's gaze with unwavering intensity. "Five to settle his debt. Another five for a promise—never sell to him again."

A hush settled over the group. The Garcias exchanged glances, unsure and calculating. The leader, eyes narrowing to assess our seriousness, gave a slight nod to one of his crew. A lanky, tattooed guy, sporting a smirk that showcased a gold tooth, sauntered over to me, clearly keen to confirm the validity of our offer.

Everyone was frozen as he meticulously counted the bills. The air around us was thick, every second stretching out like an eternity. Everyone was holding their breath, waiting for his verdict. When he finally looked up, he gave the leader a nod, indicating the amount was as promised.

"Alright," the leader growled, his voice carrying a begrudging respect. His eyes locked onto mine, a cold acknowledgment. "Consider his debt cleared. And sure, no more selling to the kid. But I want all of you off my turf. And don't think about coming back."

The Garcia gang stepped aside, providing a clear path to our vehicle. I could feel their eyes drilling holes into our backs as we made our way, cautious but trying not to seem so. Becca was the first to slide into the car, her hands trembling as she tried to buckle up. I carried Mikey, setting him in the back and buckling him in.

I climbed in after her, my eyes continuously darting to the rear-view mirror to ensure we weren't being followed. The engine roared to life, and the SUV began its journey out of that godforsaken place.

As we drove, an oppressive silence blanketed the car. The gravity of what had just transpired was palpable. Every one of us was deeply immersed in our own thoughts, processing the risks, the choices, and the narrow escape.

Just when I thought the silence would be unbroken for the entirety of the drive, Mikey groaned softly, his eyes fluttering open, displaying a confused and cloudy expression.

The weight in the car shifted, everyone's focus directed toward him.

"What the hell happened?" he asked.

Becca's face, which had previously been a mask of strain and worry, broke into pure relief. She reached over, her fingers brushing back the unruly hair from Mikey's forehead, her voice shaky but filled with affection, "Thank God, Mikey... thank God."

CHAPTER 35

BECCA

The next day, the air in the living room was thick with tension. It felt as though everyone was holding their breath. We were all waiting for any update on Mikey, anxious to know if he was alright. The only sounds were the ticking of the ornate grandfather clock by the doorway and the occasional shuffling of feet.

Then, after what felt like an eternity, the sound of footsteps echoed from above. A woman descended the staircase, her presence demanding immediate attention. She was tall with strong posture and an air of authority. Her jet-black hair was pulled back into a tight bun, emphasizing her sharp cheekbones and piercing blue eyes. The white coat she wore highlighted her mocha skin, and her lips were set in a straight line, revealing no emotion. Her aura radiated total competence and control.

Dr. Hendricks was the private MD the guys had hired the night before to check on Mikey so we didn't have to take him to the hospital. It hadn't been easy to get a doctor here on Christmas Eve, but the guys had made it happen.

Everyone in the room turned their attention to her, each one silently urging her to share good news. For a moment, her gaze flicked over each of us, as if assessing how to deliver her message. Then she cleared her throat.

"He's still stable," she began, her voice a calming blend of professionalism and warmth. "I've run some tests, and it appears he didn't ingest a lethal amount. He'll need a lot of rest, and I'll recommend rehab and counseling... but he should recover."

I hadn't realized I'd been gripping the armrest so tightly until I felt the pain in my fingers. The relief flooded through me was so overwhelming I couldn't contain it. Tears spilled down my cheeks, a torrent of emotions crashing over me all at once: gratitude, love, fear, relief.

The guys were by my side in an instant, their familiar touches wrapping around me like a protective shield. Luke's fingers brushed a stray tear from my cheek, Archer squeezed my hand reassuringly, Isaac whispered soothing words, and Vinnie wrapped an arm around my shoulders. Their collective warmth, the comfort they offered, made the weight of the past hours seem just a bit lighter.

"I don't know how I'd have made it without you guys," I said through my tears. The words felt inadequate to capture the depth of my gratitude, but I hoped they conveyed the essence.

The room had a quiet intensity that seemed to draw the walls a little tighter around us. I could feel it, a thick strain building, holding us in place. It was inescapable.

"I checked on Mikey earlier, when he first woke up," Mom began, her voice soft yet firm, drawing everyone's attention. "Our talk was short, but we agreed he's going to stay here for the time being. He needs love and family, and you, my dear," Mom nodded to me. "You need a break from being your brother's keeper."

I swallowed, feeling the familiar pang of guilt and worry. But deep down, I knew it was for the best. "That's a good decision," I replied, nodding. "He doesn't have access to drugs here. The guys made sure of that."

Sal cleared his throat, signaling a shift in the conversation to the topic I'd been both anticipating and dreading. "About this... relationship," he started, his gaze flitting across each of our faces, lingering slightly longer on his sons. "This is not what I envisioned for you," he said, with a hint of sadness.

There was a pause, the weight of his words sinking in. It was clear he had been reflecting on this, perhaps even losing sleep over it.

"When I looked to the future, I imagined each of my sons," his gaze softened as it met Isaac's, silently including him, "with a beautiful, loving woman by his side. I pictured weddings, children – grandkids running around."

Mom took up where Sal left off, her eyes glassy with unshed tears. "And for you, Becca," she said, her gaze steady on me. "I hoped for a doting husband, someone who cherished you. And, of course, beautiful grandbabies for me to spoil."

I opened my mouth to reply, to try and assuage their concerns, or maybe just to defend our choices. But before I could get a word out, Mom raised her hand, signaling for me to stop. Vinnie tried to interject as well, but Sal's firm voice cut him off.

"We're not done," he said simply.

Sal released a deep sigh, and for a moment, he looked older, the lines on his face deepening with emotion. "But," he began, his voice gentler now, "while this situation is...

unorthodox," he glanced at Mom, who nodded, "Mary and I can't deny what we see."

He looked pointedly at each of his sons, and I could see the love in his eyes. "The way you all look at Becca... the way you move around her, always making sure she's safe and cared for... It's evident. And the way you all looked out for each other during this situation with Mikey, it's clear to me. You love her. And you," he said, turning to me, "the way you stand with them, support them, it's clear. This is not a fleeting fling for you either."

Mom took a deep breath, her hand searching for Sal's. Finding it, she intertwined her fingers with his, drawing strength from the contact. "All any parent can ask for is for their child to be happy, safe, and loved," she began, her voice quivering ever so slightly.

Sal nodded in agreement, taking over the conversation. "This isn't easy for us, you know," he said, sweeping his gaze over all of us. "The idea of stepsiblings in a romantic relationship, it's unfamiliar. To be frank, it feels wrong."

My heart caught in my throat. For a brief moment, I allowed myself to imagine the worst, that they'd demand we end things or that they'd ostracize us. "But yesterday you said you'd support us," I reminded them.

"And we do," Sal promised.

"We've thought about this, long and hard," Mom said softly. "We've decided not to marry."

The room went still. For a second, I couldn't comprehend what she'd just said. "What? Why?" I blurted out. The weight of everything, from Mikey to our relationship, bore down on me, and now this? It was too much. "You love each other. You should be together. This shouldn't change anything."

Vinnie jumped in, his voice a mix of exasperation and

disbelief. "This is ridiculous. You two belong together. Just because we're with Becca doesn't make her our sister. It's not the same. You shouldn't have to sacrifice your happiness for us."

Isaac and Archer nodded in agreement, their faces a mirror of Vinnie's emotions.

Luke nodded as well and added, "You've both found a second chance at love. It's rare. Don't throw it away."

Mom looked teary-eyed, while Sal appeared deep in thought. "It's not just about what society thinks," she whispered. "It's about what's right for our family."

"But Mom," I pleaded, my voice breaking, "it's your happiness. You both deserve that. You've been through so much. Don't let this be another sacrifice."

Vinnie wrapped an arm around me, pulling me close, echoing my sentiments. "She's right. You should marry, be happy. We'll deal with the rest."

There was a profound silence. The weight of our words, our entreaties, filled the room. I could see the conflict in Mom's eyes, the desire to be with Sal warring with her maternal instincts to protect her family, to ensure our happiness.

Sal sighed, running a hand through his hair. "We never wanted any of this to get in the way of our love, or yours," he said, looking at each of us in turn. "We just want what's best."

"We all do," I whispered, wiping away a tear. "But maybe what's best is for all of us to be happy. Together."

The room was silent for a moment, the weight of their words sinking in. Sal and Mom exchanged one of those looks filled with a silent understanding and agreement before Mom cleared her throat and spoke.

"We're already married here," she said, placing a hand

over her heart. "We don't need a piece of paper to tell us that. Love is about commitment, understanding, and being there for each other, in every situation. We have that. We don't need society's stamp to affirm our bond."

Sal nodded in agreement. "And if the five of you can't get legally married, even if that's where your hearts lead you, then maybe this is a way for all of us to stand against the conventional norms together."

I felt a rush of emotion, tears pooling in my eyes as I dashed forward, embracing my mom. "I just want you to be happy," I whispered into her hair.

"We are happy, and we will be happy for a very long time," Mom reassured us.

Sal and the guys shared a series of warm, back-slapping hugs, the bond of brotherhood evident. Vinnie clapped Sal on the back, his eyes moist, and even Archer, usually so reserved, pulled Sal into a tight embrace.

The warmth in the room was palpable, the love evident in every shared glance and touch. There was a feeling of unity, of togetherness that seemed to wrap around all of us, holding us close. It was as if an unspoken understanding had passed between us all, a commitment to each other and to our unconventional, yet beautiful, family.

Mom broke the tender moment with her infectious, heartwarming laughter. "In all of the, um, excitement, we almost forgot it's Christmas Eve." She clapped her hands together excitedly, her face beaming. "And, if I may say so myself, I've already received the most wonderful gift I could have ever asked for: a big, loving family to celebrate with."

Sal's eyes twinkled as he pulled Mom close. "Here's to new beginnings and to celebrating love in all its beautiful forms."

The room resonated with a chorus of agreement. Wine

glasses clinked, and we toasted to love, to family, and to a future filled with promise. Despite the hurdles, uncertainties, and challenges that lay ahead, in that moment, everything felt just right. The house echoed with laughter, joy, and love – the essence of a true family Christmas.

Three days later...

The spirit of Christmas, with its warmth and enchantment, had always held a special place in my heart. But this Christmas, it carried an even deeper meaning. The love that filled the room, the acceptance from Sal and Mom, and the undeniable bond we all shared had turned an ordinary festive season into something profoundly magical.

Sal and Mom's decision to prioritize our happiness, to stand beside us as we navigated the intricacies of our unorthodox relationship, was a testament to their unwavering love and support. Their sacrifice not only showcased the depth of their feelings for us but also solidified my own feelings. It dawned on me that, for the first time, there was no hesitation in my heart. I was ready to dive deep, to commit to this relationship, to these incredible men who had become my life.

But as fate would have it, the universe had another surprise in store for me. The morning after the euphoria of

Christmas, as the remnants of wrapping paper and bows still littered the living room, I stared at the two pink lines on the pregnancy test, my heart pounding in my chest.

I was pregnant.

A flood of emotions overtook me. Excitement, anxiety, happiness, and trepidation blended into a whirlwind inside me. The weight of the news was heavy, yet the prospect of carrying our love, a tangible symbol of our commitment, was intoxicating. I felt grateful, and a tiny bit overwhelmed.

But while my heart rejoiced, a nagging thought lingered. How would the guys react? Sure, they loved me, and we had already weathered many storms together. But a child? That was a commitment of an entirely different magnitude.

In the days that followed, I wrestled with my emotions. The joy of the holiday season was intermingled with my own internal conflict. On one hand, Mikey's condition added a layer of complexity. His brush with the abyss, the toll of his drug use, was a painful reminder of how fragile life could be.

But he was already showing signs of recovery. He'd come to on Christmas morning, feeling well enough for a little hot cider. The light was slowly returned to his eyes, and by the morning after Christmas, he seemed to be regaining some semblance of his old self. Knowing I'd be leaving him in the caring hands of Mom and Sal was no small relief.

Before leaving, I confided in Mom about the pregnancy. She hugged me tight, tears glistening in her eyes.

"This is a gift, Becca. A blessing." I made her swear not to tell the guys, though I gave her permission to share the news with Sal. Some things were too precious, too important to be kept from those we loved.

We'd left that next day. And as the guys' private plane soared through the clear blue sky, taking us back to New York, I felt the weight of the secret pressing on me. It was time. I had to tell them.

The ambiance inside the plane was light, with sporadic bouts of laughter and playful banter. The guys seemed relaxed, enjoying the luxury of the plush leather seats and the panoramic views outside. But as I looked at each of them — Vinnie with his charming smile, Archer enjoying a glass of his usual red wine, Isaac, calm and collected, and Luke already getting started on work for the new year — I felt a pang of nervousness.

With a wistful smile, I gazed at them, thinking how incredibly lucky I was. They seemed to be radiating an irresistible charm today, each in their own unique way.

Vinnie caught my gaze first, his dark eyes twinkling mischievously. "Like what you see?" he teased, flexing his arm muscles in an exaggerated gesture.

I feigned shock, placing a hand over my heart. "Oh my! I might just faint from the sheer overwhelming display of machismo!"

Archer chuckled from my left, leaning in closer to whisper in my ear, his warm breath sending a tingling sensation down my spine. "I think you're just flustered because we keep getting better with age. Like fine wine."

Grinning, I turned toward him, placing a finger under his chin. "Oh, Archer, honey, while you definitely age like wine, I think Vinnie's more like cheese. Some might say he's...aged to perfection?"

Luke leaned in and smoothly interjected, "Careful, Becca. With all these compliments, you might just inflate our egos to an unsustainable size."

Winking at him, I quipped, "Wouldn't dream of it. Just

calling it as I see it. I mean, seriously, did you guys make a pact with the devil or something? It's like you become more irresistible by the day."

Vinnie smirked. "Maybe it's all that love from you. It has rejuvenating properties, you know."

I laughed. "Well, in that case, you'll all be forever young."

"Or," Archer added with a roguish grin, "it's just the effect you have on us. Keeps us on our toes, keeps the blood pumping. Good for the complexion, you know?"

Rolling my eyes playfully, I retorted, "Nice try. I'm pretty sure it's just your genes. But if you're trying to butter me up, it's working."

Isaac leaned in, his blue eyes soft yet intense. "You know, we might be a good-looking bunch," he started, his voice dripping with mock arrogance, "but there's a particular lady here whose beauty steals the show every single time."

Blushing slightly, I swatted him lightly on the arm. "Oh, stop. This isn't a competition, you know. Besides, surrounded by all of you, how could I not glow a little?"

Vinnie pretended to ponder for a moment. "I have a theory," he mused. "We're all just reflections. We shine because you shine."

Archer snorted and smirked. "Deep, Vinnie. Real deep."

Chuckling, I shook my head at their antics. "All I know is, I'm one lucky girl to have such...visually pleasing company. And even luckier that you all have personalities to match those devilish good looks."

Isaac smirked, capturing my hand and placing a gentle kiss on the back. "Well, remember, you're the gem that completes this dashing ensemble."

The warmth in the cabin was unmistakable, filled with

lighthearted laughter, flirtatious exchanges, and a bond that was only growing stronger.

Surrounded by the luxurious trappings of the private plane, I could feel the tension of desire in the air. It wasn't just the altitude; being enclosed in this exclusive space with the four men I adored most was heady and intoxicating.

"Gentlemen," I began, a sly grin forming on my lips, "as much as I would love to christen this plane properly with each of you, I think patience is a virtue worth practicing." I let my fingers brush past Archer's thigh and winked at Vinnie, delighting in their collective groans.

Truth be told, I was way, way too nervous about the pregnancy news to be thinking about sex. I mean, I was *always* thinking about sex when I was around the guys – how could I not? But the news was so intense, so earth-shattering, it temporarily eclipsed my desire for them.

Isaac's penthouse in Midtown Manhattan was nothing short of a masterpiece. The vast living space was adorned with floor-to-ceiling windows that boasted a panoramic view of the New York skyline. Rich mahogany accents, plush furnishings, and a minimalist design exuded opulence. An open-concept kitchen with sleek black granite countertops glistened under the soft, ambient lighting. Every inch of the place radiated luxury and elegance, fitting for the man who owned it.

"Now, this isn't *my* place," Isaac said as he took my bag. "Why don't you move in with us, assuming that's what you want?"

I grinned. "Nothing would make me happier."

After exploring every nook and cranny of the opulent space, we settled into the cozy living area. It was evening, the city lights painting a picturesque backdrop. The topic of conversation shifted to our futures, which seemed more intertwined than ever.

"I've been thinking," Isaac began, his deep voice capturing our attention. "This place is big enough for all of us – not just Becca and me. What do you all say about making this our home?"

Vinnie nodded in agreement. "It's the perfect place to start our life together."

Archer chimed in, "It's practical and beautiful. Plus, with all of us here, we can truly make it ours."

Feeling a burst of joy at the thought of a shared future, I interjected, "I'm all in. Living together sounds perfect."

"More than room enough for five," Luke said.

Make that six, I thought. The tension building inside me was nearly too much. I had to tell the guys, and it couldn't wait a minute longer. With the important decision made, I took a deep breath, preparing to share some surprises of my own.

"Alright, now that we've settled that, I have two surprises for you all."

Reaching into my bag, I brought out the first gift – framed photographs of the majestic stallions I'd captured during our time at the cabin. Their sheer power and grace were frozen in time, a perfect reflection of the men before me.

"These are incredible, Becca," Archer whispered, clearly moved by the sentiment.

Vinnie added, holding his frame close, "A beautiful reminder of our time together. Thank you."

Holding out a small Christmas sack, I teased, "There's one more surprise. But there's a catch. Only one of you can open it."

The guys exchanged glances, each contemplating

whether to take the lead. After a playful round of rock-paper-scissors, Isaac emerged the victor.

With a playful smirk, I handed him the sack, "Go on. This surprise is for all of you."

Isaac carefully untied the ribbon and reached inside. Pulling out a tiny pair of baby shoes, he looked up, his eyes searching mine for confirmation. The rest of the room was in stunned silence.

"I'm pregnant," I whispered, my heart swelling with emotion.

In the immediate aftermath of the words tumbling from my lips, a heavy silence settled in the room. The weight of my confession, the enormity of it, hung in the air, making it dense, almost suffocating. For a split second, I wondered if I'd made the right decision in telling them here, in this grand penthouse overlooking the heart of Manhattan.

And then, the reactions came in a cascade of emotions.

Vinnie was the first to break the silence, his face lighting up in a broad grin. "We're going to be dads? All of us?"

Luke, ever the practical one, immediately wanted details. "Have you seen a doctor?"

Archer knelt in front of me, placing a gentle hand over my still-flat belly. "There's a little life in there," he whispered, his eyes moist with emotion.

Isaac simply pulled me into a tight embrace, burying his face in my hair. "Thank you," he murmured. "For this gift."

"I haven't seen the doctor yet," I said. "I go in two weeks and you can all come with me if you want."

The room was awash in a mixture of excitement, anticipation, and a dash of nervousness. Champagne was poured -sparkling cider for me- glasses clinked, and plans were immediately hatched. We discussed baby rooms, name choices, and all the responsibilities that come with a newborn. It was clear that each one of them was already deeply invested in this new life, ready to face the challenges and joys of fatherhood.

I watched them, these strong, powerful men, each expressing their joy and commitment in their unique ways. I was struck by the beauty of the moment, the confluence of our love creating a new chapter in our lives.

The warmth from our celebration, the thrill of our impending parenthood, everything mingled, creating an electricity in the room. The joy from the news of the pregnancy had somehow evolved into a *different* kind of excitement, one I was familiar with when I was around my men.

The light banter and teasing shifted subtly, eyes deepening with desire, touches lingering a little longer, and before I was even conscious of how it began, clothes began to shed. The opulence of Isaac's penthouse seemed to fade into insignificance as I became the center of their universe.

The silk of the carpet against my back was cool, but the heat from the hands caressing me was more than enough to keep the chill at bay. Archer's lips were on mine, passionate but tender, as if he were savoring the news just shared. Luke was at my ear, his whispers not words, but breathy sighs, letting me know without words what he intended.

Archer's hands, always so confident, began to explore me. His fingertips danced down my sides, sending shivers up my spine, then tracing patterns over my stomach, before settling where I ached the most. The intimacy of his touch, combined with the depth of our emotional connection, had me spiraling quickly.

At the same time, Luke focused on my upper body, his lips kissing a hot path down my neck to my breasts, where he lavished attention. The sensation of his mouth and Archer's hands working in tandem was overwhelming. Luke looked up, locking eyes with me as he increased the intensity of his attentions, challenging me to hold his gaze.

It wasn't long before Luke's dedication and Archer's insistent touch pushed me past the point of no return. I felt the wave building and then crashing over me, my body arching off the floor as I was lost in the sensation. I could feel both of them react to my release — Luke from the way my body tightened around his fingers and Archer from the sounds I couldn't restrain.

As my own climax washed over me, I could sense both of them reaching their peaks. Archer moved inside me as Luke took his hand away, and after a few deep thrusts his eyes held a fiery passion, and I could feel the tremors of his release even as he continued to prioritize my pleasure. Luke, with his lips still locked onto my skin, his manhood inside my mouth, let out a muffled groan, signaling his surrender to the moment. We came together, the three of us rising and crashing at once.

I grinned as I gazes at the handsome men around me. Nice thing about having four lovers was how there was always at least one man eager to please you. Lovemaking with them was an endless cascade of pleasure, each of them craving the sight of my release.

As Luke and Archer disentangled themselves and laid back to catch their breath, I felt Vinnie's presence behind me. His firm, steady hands gripped my waist, pulling me onto all fours. His whispers, husky and deep, promised a pleasure that left me breathless with anticipation. Vinnie had this uncanny ability to convey passion and desire with the simplest touch, and I was ready for him.

With one strong thrust, Vinnie glided inside me. My body welcomed him, adjusting to his size and rhythm. With each thrust, he took me closer and closer to the edge. The sensation of him moving inside me, coupled with the lingering tremors from my previous release, had me spiraling quickly. His pace intensified, every movement calculated and deliberate, until he hit the spot, that sweet, magical spot that sent a jolt of electricity through me, ending in a thundering climax that seemed to last forever.

As Vinnie and I both came down from our respective highs, Isaac made his presence known. With Vinnie's warmth still lingering, Isaac laid me down gently on my back, his intense eyes never leaving mine. He hovered above me, our breaths mingling, our lips just a whisper apart. And then he was kissing me, stealing my breath and my thoughts.

Isaac's lovemaking was always a dance of passion and intimacy. There was an urgency to it, but also a tenderness that spoke of the depth of our connection. He entered me smoothly, setting a rhythm that had me gasping and clutching at the sheets beneath me. Every thrust, every touch, every kiss was a testament to the love we shared.

The world seemed to narrow down to just the two of us. The feel of him moving within me, stretching me out, the taste of his lips on mine, the sound of our moans mixing with the distant hum of the city - it was all-consuming. With a final, shared climax, we surrendered to the intensity of the moment.

When it was all said and done, we lay there, intertwined and spent, gazing out over the magnificent New York skyline. Vinnie draped an arm over my waist, his breath tickling the nape of my neck. Luke and Archer, their warmth seeping into me from either side, held me close. And Isaac, ever the protector, lay above us all, shielding and watching.

The city lights twinkled, each one holding a promise of

a future filled with magic, love, and infinite possibilities. We were on the cusp of a new journey, with challenges and joys we couldn't even begin to imagine. But in that moment, in the quiet intimacy of Isaac's penthouse, I knew one thing for certain — no matter what the future held, it was ours to share.

EPILOGUE II

ISAAC

A little under one year later...

Christmas always had a way of making things feel a little more alive. But this year? This year was special. We were celebrating in our new home, a sprawling estate nestled in Fairhaven, a quaint little town in upstate New York. And when I say sprawling, I mean the house stretched on forever, a testament to the combined ambitions of four determined men.

I still couldn't get over the magnificent mansion we called home. I remember the day we first laid eyes on it, the regal, stone facade framed by towering oak trees. The place boasted more bedrooms than we knew what to do with, every one of them spacious, oozing luxury and style.

The gourmet kitchen, with its state-of-the-art appliances and a marbled island that seemed to stretch for miles, was Becca's favorite. She had dreams of putting her skills to the test, cooking feasts and hosting parties, with us hovering around, stealing bites and kisses.

But as much as we loved our charming upstate haven, we couldn't give up the energy of the city. So, we held onto our Manhattan penthouse, a tether to the buzz of our work lives and the fast-paced world we occasionally craved. After all, FourSight wasn't going to run itself.

The sound of a car pulling up jerked me from my reminiscences. Peeking through the frost-kissed window, I saw Mary and Sal stepping out, their arms loaded with presents and bags of what I assumed were holiday treats. The old man looked up, his eyes finding mine, and he winked. That wink spoke volumes — of approval, of acceptance, of understanding.

As the door swung open, the cold winter air mixed with the warmth of the house, carrying with it the intoxicating aroma of pine, roasted chestnuts, and the subtle scent of cinnamon. Mary, always lively, burst through the door first, her voice ringing out in joyous greeting.

"Merry Christmas, everyone!"

Sal followed suit, his more restrained demeanor balancing out Mary's exuberance. "Good to see you all," he said, casting an appreciative glance around the grand entrance hall.

Becca rushed forward, enveloping her mother in a tight embrace. The bond between them had only grown stronger over the last year. As for Sal, he received a bear hug from each one of us.

"We couldn't let you guys start Christmas without us," Mary declared, her eyes twinkling with mischief.

"I wouldn't dream of it," Becca replied with a laugh. "I love this place, but man, would it feel empty without family. And we've still got two more days before Christmas."

Mary's eyes flashed with excitement. "And where's the little lady?"

Becca smiled warmly in the way she always did when our daughter was mentioned. "Sleeping. Don't worry, she'll be up soon."

"Good! Because do I have presents for her or what!"

"We come bearing gifts," Sal said with a smile. "Go check the completely full trunk of the car if you don't believe me."

I watched the scene unfold, a deep contentment settling within me. This was what life was all about: the moments spent with loved ones, creating memories that would last a lifetime.

We settled in, and the gentle hum of conversations, the clink of ice against glass, and the subtle background of Sinatra's crooning -Sal's pick, of course- filled our expansive living room. I sat, relishing the full-bodied taste of the bourbon in my glass, Sal and my brothers, Vinnie, Luke, and Archer, deep in discussion about the latest in marketing trends. Becca and Mary caught up on all the family goings on before moving on to discussing plans for decorating the rest of the huge house. The warmth of the room, aided by the crackling fireplace and towering tree, made me appreciate how far we'd all come, how tightly knit our bond had grown.

And it wasn't long before my thoughts drifted to the other most important girl in my life.

Our little Madeline, just three months old, had quickly become the heart and soul of our home. Maddie, as we fondly called her, had Becca's bright hazel eyes and a sprinkle of auburn hair atop her head that gleamed in sunlight, suggesting it might deepen to match my own. Each day seemed to bring a new development, a new expression, or a fresh sound from her. She was a perfect blend of her mother and all of us, and I found myself often marveling at the wonder of life, and how something so small and delicate could wield such power over four grown men.

As if on cue, the soft chiming of the baby monitor stirred me from my thoughts. Madeline's coos and gurgles indicated she was awake from her nap. Without missing a beat, Luke, Archer, Vinnie, and I converged on her room. Becca got there first, lifting Maddie from her crib. As those little arms reached out, her small fingers wrapping around Becca's thumb, we all gathered around, a protective and adoring circle.

Vinnie made silly faces, earning a bubbly giggle from Maddie. Archer softly hummed a tune, while Luke gently stroked her cheek. I leaned in, planting a soft kiss on her forehead, absorbing the warmth and innocent love radiating from her. This was family, a bond unbreakable, built on love and commitment. This was our forever.

After a quick diaper change, Maddie came down with us, and it wasn't long before Grandma Mary and Nonno Sal were doting on her like crazy, the little girl enjoying the attention with a big smile on her face.

Lost in my thoughts, I was drawn back to reality by the soft shuffle of footsteps. Vinnie walked into the kitchen, where the soft murmur of Becca's voice indicated she was on a call. He paused briefly at the threshold, his brows furrowing as he observed her. The usual vibrant lilt in her voice was missing, replaced with a somber tone that immediately set off alarm bells in my mind.

"What's wrong?" Vinnie mouthed, trying to gauge the situation.

Becca held up a finger, signaling him to wait. Trusting Vinnie to handle things in the kitchen, I focused my attention on Sal, who was in the middle of playing peek-a-boo with Maddie.

But soon, the narrative faded into the background as Luke, Archer, and I noticed Vinnie carefully assembling the charcuterie board Becca had left half-finished. Her silence and his actions told us all we needed to know—something was amiss.

The three of us ventured into the kitchen, our steps in sync, a protective circle forming instinctively around the woman who held the center of our universe. Becca finished her call and for a long moment simply stared into the distance, her thoughts clearly miles away.

The weight of silence bore down on all of us until she finally looked up, her gaze capturing each of ours. A soft, sad smile played on her lips, instantly telling us that whatever news she had wasn't all bad. "That was Mikey," she began, her voice breaking slightly.

I felt Vinnie's tension. But all of us stayed silent, giving her the space to continue.

"He... he apologized for everything." She paused, gathering herself. We all remembered the tumultuous few months that followed that fateful Christmas Eve. Mikey had put us all through the wringer with his substance issues, his actions nearly fracturing the tight bond our family shared. "He's been clean eight months now."

A collective sigh of relief passed between us, the cloud of worry lifting ever so slightly. Her next words, however, captured our attention.

"He wants to come for Christmas, to meet Madeline."

The room's atmosphere shifted. A myriad of emotions swept over us—hesitation, uncertainty, hope. Mikey, for all his faults, was still family. And Madeline, our beautiful daughter, was the symbol of the love, resilience, and unity our family stood for.

My brothers and I exchanged glances. We had a decision to make. And as we did with every major choice in our life, we would make it together.

I smiled. "We can send the plane tomorrow. He can come in and be here by Christmas Eve dinner."

Becca's eyes, glossy with tears of joy, shone brightly as they danced from one of us to the next. The raw emotion, the sheer depth of feeling in the room, was palpable. We all felt it—the completeness, the sense of belonging, the realization that we had each other, always.

"This is wonderful news, Becca," I said, feeling a surge of pride and love for her. She had been our rock, the glue that held us together, and it felt fitting that she'd be the one to bring Mikey back into the fold. We all knew how much she'd struggled with his absence.

"I've never been happier," she whispered, wiping away a tear that had escaped.

Vinnie shot me a knowing glance, his eyes twinkling with mischief. I couldn't help but smirk in return, our shared secret burning between us. But our silent exchange didn't go unnoticed.

"What's going on?" Luke inquired, looking between the two of us with raised eyebrows. "Are you guys thinking..."

"Is now a good time?" Archer chimed in, already aware of what we had planned.

Becca's gaze flitted between us all, confusion evident in her features. "What are you guys up to?"

Before she could inquire further, Vinnie reached into his pocket, producing a slim, shimmering band. "Becca," he began, his voice laden with emotion, "From the moment I met you, I knew you were the missing piece in my life. I love you more than words can express." He slid the band onto her finger.

I stepped forward next, another identical band in hand.

Looking deep into her eyes, I whispered, "For every sunrise we've watched together, and for every sunset we've yet to see, my love for you grows. This is my promise to cherish and love you forever." I slid my band next to Vinnie's, the two fitting together seamlessly.

Luke was next, his tone soft yet unwavering. "Every moment, every laugh, every tear we've shared... I cherish them all. I want a lifetime more with you." His band fit snugly next to mine.

Finally, Archer stepped up, his band gleaming in his hand. "Becca, you've brought light, love, and laughter into my life. I promise to give you the same for all our days to come." And he slid his band onto her finger, completing the quartet.

"The bands," Luke began, seeing the wonder in Becca's eyes, "were crafted specially for you. They fit together, just like we do. While we can't marry you in the conventional sense, this is our way of committing to you. Forever."

Becca looked down at her hand, the bands shimmering in the soft light, each one a testament to the love of the man who had given it to her. Tears flowed anew, but this time, they were tears of pure, unadulterated joy.

"I love you all," she whispered, her voice thick with emotion. "More than you'll ever know."

One by one, we took her in our arms, sealing our promises with soft, lingering kisses. The world outside faded away, leaving just the five of us in our shared cocoon of love and happiness.

And as we stood there, wrapped up in each other, the future stretched out before us—full of promise, full of love, and full of the magic that came from finding your true place in the world.

The End

Printed in Great Britain
by Amazon